I0784632

James Lane Allen

THE DOCTOR'S CHRISTMAS EVE

OK Publishing 2021

James Lane Allen

THE DOCTOR'S CHRISTMAS EVE

A Moving Saga of a Man's Journey through His Life

Published by

MUSAICUM

Books

Advanced Digital Solutions & High-Quality book Formatting
musaicumbooks@okpublishing.info

2021 OK Publishing

ISBN 978-80-272-7624-0

Contents

Part I

I. The Children of Desire

The morning of the twenty-fourth of December a quarter of a century ago opened upon the vast plateau of central Kentucky as a brilliant but bitter day-with a wind like the gales of March.

Out in a neighborhood of one of the wealthiest and most thickly settled counties, toward the middle of the forenoon, two stumpy figures with movements full of health and glee appeared on a hilltop of the treeless landscape. They were the children of the neighborhood physician, a man of the highest consequence in his part of the world; and they had come from their home, a white and lemon-colored eighteenth-century manor house a mile in their rear. Through the crystalline air the chimneys of this low structure, rising out of a green girdle of cedar trees, could be seen emptying unusual smoke which the wind in its gambolling pounced upon and jerked away level with the chimney-tops.

But if you had stood on the hill where the two children climbed into view and if your eye could have swept round the horizon with adequate radius of vision, it would everywhere have been greeted by the same wondrous harmonious spectacle: out of the chimneys of all dwellings scattered in comfort and permanence over that rich domestic land —a land of Anglo-Saxon American homes-more than daily winter smoke was pouring: one spirit of preparation, one mood of good will, warmed houses and hearts. The whole visible heaven was receiving the incense of Kentucky Christmas fires; the whole visible earth was a panorama of the common peace.

The two dauntless, frost-defying wayfarers-what Emerson, meeting them in the depths of a New England winter, might have called two scraps of valor-were following across fields and meadows and pastures one of the footpaths which children who are friendly neighbors naturally make in order to get to each other, as the young of wild creatures trace for themselves upon the earth some new map of old hereditary traits and cravings. For the goal of their journey they were hurrying toward a house not yet in sight but hardly more than a mile ahead, where they were to spend Christmas Day and share in an old people's and children's Christmas-Tree party on Christmas Night-and where also they were to put into execution a plot of their own: about which a good deal is to be narrated.

They were thus transferring the nation's yearly festival of the home from their own roof-tree to that of another family as the place where it could be enacted and enjoyed. The tragical meaning of this arrangement was but too well understood by their parents. To them the abandonment of their own fireside at the season when its bonds should have been freshened and deepened scarcely seemed an unnatural occurrence. The other house had always been to them as a secondary home. It was the residence of their father's friend, a professor in the State University situated some miles off across fine country. His two surviving children, a boy and a girl of about their own ages, had always been their intimate associates. And the woman of that household-the wife, the mother-all their lives they had been mysteriously impelled toward this gentlewoman by a power of which they were unconscious but by which they had been swayed.

The little girl wore a crimson hood and a brown cloak and the boy a crimson skull cap and a brown overcoat; and both wore crimson mittens; and both were red-legged and red-footed; for stockings had been drawn over their boots to insure warmth and to provide safeguard against slipping when they should cross the frozen Elkhorn or venture too friskily on silvery pools in the valley bottoms.

The chestnut braids of the girl falling heavily from under her hood met in a loop in the middle of her broad fat back and were tied there with a snip of ribbon that looked like a feather out of the wing of a bluejay. Her bulging hips overreached the borders of the narrow path, so that the boy was crowded out upon the rough ground as he struggled forward close beside her. She would not allow him to walk in front of her and he disdained to walk behind.

"Then walk beside me or go back!" she had said to him, laughing carelessly.

She looked so tight inside her wrappings, so like a jolly ambulatory small barrel well hooped and mischievously daubed here and there with vermilion, that you might have had misgivings as to the fate of the barrel, were it to receive a violent jolt and be rolled over. No thought of such mishap troubled her as she trotted forward, balancing herself as lightly on her cushioned feet as though she were wind-carried thistledown. Nor was she disturbed by her selfishness in monopolizing the path and forcing her brother to encounter whatsoever the winter earth obtruded-stumps of forest trees, brambles of blackberry, sprouts of cane, or stalks of burdock and of Spanish needle. His footing was especially troublesome when he tried to straddle wide corn-rows with his short legs; or when they crossed a hemp-field where the butt-ends of the stalks serried the frost-gray soil like bayonet points. Altogether his exertions put him out of breath somewhat, for his companion was fleet and she made no allowance for his delays and difficulties.

Her hands, deep in the fleece-lined mittens, were comfortably warm; but she moreover kept them thrust into a muff of white fur, which also looked overfed and seemed of a gay harmony with its owner. This muff she now and then struck against her flexed knees in a vixenish play-fulness as one beats a tambourine on a bent elbow; and at a certain point of the journey, having glanced sidewise at him and remarked his breath on the icy air, she lifted it to her mouth and spoke guardedly from behind it: —

"Remember the last thing Papa told us at the window, Herbert: we were to keep our mouths closed and to breathe through our noses. And remember also, my child, that we were to rely upon —*especially* to rely upon-the ribs and the diaphragm! I wonder why he thought it necessary to tell us that! Did he suppose that as soon as we got by ourselves or arrived at the Ousleys', we'd begin to rely upon something else, and perhaps try to breathe with our spines and elbows?"

Her eyes sparkled with mischief, and her laughter had the audacity of a child's satire, often more terrible in its small world than a sage's in his larger one. The instant she spoke, you recognized the pertness and precocity of an American child-which, when seen at its best or at its worst, is without precedent or parallel among the world's children. She was the image of a hard bold crisp newness. Her speech was new, her ideas were new, her impertinence was new-except in this country. She appeared to have gathered newness during her short life, to be newer than the day she was born. The air was full of frost spangles that zigzagged about her as she danced along; they rather seemed like particles of salt especially provided to escort her character. If it had been granted Lot's wife with tears of repentance to dissolve away the crystals of her curiosity and resume the duties of motherhood, —though possibly permeated by a mild saline solution as a warning, —that salt-cured matron might admirably have adapted herself to the decrees of Providence by producing Elsie.

The boy as she administered her caution stopped; and shutting his own red mouth, which was like hers though more generous, he drew a long breath through his nostrils; then, throwing back his head, he blew this out with an open-mouthed puff, and a column of white steam shot up into the blue ether and was whirled away by the wind. He stood studying it awhile as it disappeared, for he was a close observer always —a perpetual watcher of the thing that is-sometimes an observer fearful to confront. Then he sprang forward to catch up with his sharp-tongued monitress, who had hurried on. As he came alongside, he turned his face toward her and made his reply, which was certainly deliberate enough in arriving: —

"We have to be *taught* the best way to breathe, Elsie; as anything else!"

The defence only brought on a fresh attack: —

"I wonder who teaches the young of other animals how to breathe! I should like to know who teaches kittens and puppies and calves and lambs how to breathe! How *do* they ever manage to get along without country doctors among them! Imagine a middle-aged sheep-old Dr. Buck-assembling a flock of lambs and trying to show them how to breathe!" Judging from Elsie's expression, the lambs in the case could not have thought very highly of this queer and genial Dr. Buck.

"But *they* are all four-legged creatures, Elsie; and *they* breathe backward and forward; if you are a two-legged animal and stand up straight, you breathe up and down: it's quite different! It's easier!"

"Then I suppose the fewer legs a thing has, the harder it is to get its breath. And I suppose if we ventured to stand on *one* leg, we'd all soon suffocate! Dear me! why *don't* all one-legged people die at once!"

The lad looked over the field of war on which it would seem that he was being mowed down by small-gun fire before he could get his father's heavy artillery into action. He decided to terminate the wordy engagement, a prudential manœuvre of the wiser head but slower tongue.

"Father is right," he declared. His manner of speaking was sturdy and decisive: it was meant to remind her first that he had enough gallantry as a male to permit her to crowd him out of the path; but that the moment a struggle for mental footing arose between them, he reserved the whole road: the female could take to the weeds! He notified her also that he stood with his father not only in this puzzling question of legs and parlous types of respiration, but that the men in the family were regularly combined against the women-like good organized against evil!

But now something further had transpired. Had there been present on the winter fields that morning an ear trained to separate our complex human tones into simple ones-to disengage one from another the different fibres of meaning which always make up even the slenderest tendril of sound (as there is a cluster of grapes to a solitary stem), it might, as it noted one thing, have discovered another. While the boy asserted his father to be right in the matter they were debating, there escaped from him an accent of admission that his father was wrong-wrong in some far graver affair which was his discovery and his present trouble.

Therefore his voice, which should have been buoyant, for the instant was depressed; and his face, which should have been a healthy boy's happy face, was overcast as by a foreign interference. You might have likened it to a small luminary upon the shining disk of which a larger body, traversing its darkened orbit, has just begun to project a wavering shadow. And thus some patient astronomer of our inter-orbited lives, sweeping the spiritual heavens for signs of its pendent mysteries, here might have arrested his telescope to watch the portent of a celestial event: was there to take place the eclipse of a son by a father?

Certainly at least this weight of responsibility on the voice must have caused it to strike only the more winningly upon any hearer. It was such a devoted, loyal voice when he thus spoke of his father, with a curious quavering huskiness of its own, as though the bass note of his distant manhood were already beginning to clamor to be heard.

The voice of the little girl contrariwise was a shrill treble. Had you first become aware of it at your back, you must instantly have wheeled to investigate the small creature it came from, as a wild animal quickly turns to face any sound that startles its instincts. Voltaire might have had such a voice if he had been a little girl. Yet to look at her, you would never have imagined that anything but the honey of speech could have dripped from so perfect a little rose. (Many surprises await mankind behind round amiable female faces: shrews are not *all* thin.)

Instead of being silenced by her brother's ultimatum, she did not deign to notice it, but continued to direct her voluble satire at her father-quite with the air of saying that a girl who can satirize a parent is not to be silenced by a son.

"...forever telling us that American children must have the newest and best way of doing everything....My, my, my! The working of our jaws! And the drinking and the breathing; and the stretching and the bending: developing everything we have-and everything we haven't! I am even trying now to find an original American way to go to sleep at night and to wake up in the morning! Dear me, but old people can be silly without knowing it!" She laughed with much self-approval.

For Elsie had already entered into one of mankind's most dependable recreations-the joy of listening to our own words: into that economic arrangement of nature whereby whatsoever a human being might lose through the vocal cords is returned to the owner along the auditory nerve! So that a woman can eat her colloquial cake times over: and each time, having devoured it, can return it to the storeroom and have it brought out as whole and fresh as ever-sometimes actually increased in size. And a man can send his vocal Niagara through his whirlpool rapids and catch it again above the falls! The more gold the delver unearths, the more he can empty back into the thinking mine. One can sit in his own cranial theatre and produce his own play: he can be stage and orchestra, audience and critic; and he can see that the claque does not get drowsy and slack: it never does-in *this* case!

The child now threw back her round winter-rose of a face and started along the path with a fresh outburst of speed and pride. Access of impertinence seemed to have released in her access of vitality. Perhaps it had. Perhaps it always does. Perhaps life itself at the full is sheer audacity.

The lad scrambled roughly along, and merely repeated the words that sufficed for him: —

"Father knows."

Suddenly he gave a laughing outcry, and stood still.

"Look!" he called out, with amusement at his plight.

He had run into some burdock, and the nettles had stuck to his yarn stockings like stinging bees —a cluster of them about his knees and calves. He drew off his gloves, showing the strong, overgrown hands of boyhood: they, like his voice, seemed impatiently reaching out for maturity.

When he overtook his companion, who had not stopped, he had transferred a few of the burrs to his skull cap. He had done this with crude artistry-from some faint surviving impulse of primitive man to decorate his body with things around him in nature: especially his head (possibly he foresaw that his head would be most struck at). The lad was pleased with his caper; and, smiling, thrust his head across her path, expecting her to take sympathetic notice. He had reason to expect this, because on dull rainy days at home he often amused her with the things he did and the things he made: for he was a natural carpenter and toy-maker. But now she took only the contemptuous notice of disapproval. This morning her mind was intent on playthings of positive value: she was a little travelling ten-toed pagoda of holiday greed. Every Christmas she prepared for its celebration with a balancing eye to what it would cost her and what it would bring in: she always calculated to receive more than she gave: for Elsie, the Nativity must be made *to pay*!

He resented her refusal to approve his playfulness by so much as a smile, and he came back at her by doing worse: —

"Why didn't I think to bring all the burrs along and make a Christmas basket for Elizabeth? Now what will I give her?"

This drew out a caustic comment quickly enough: —

"Poor Elizabeth!"

A child resents injustice with a blow or rage or tears: the old have learned to endure without a sign-waiting for God's day of judgment (or their first good opportunity!).

He was furious at the way she said "Poor Elizabeth" —as though Elizabeth's hands would be empty of gifts from him.

"You *know* I have *bought* my presents for Elizabeth, Elsie!" he exclaimed. "But Elizabeth thinks more of what I *make* than of what I *buy*," he continued hotly. "And the less it is worth, the more she values it. But you can't understand *that*, Elsie! And you needn't try!"

The little minx laughed with triumph that she had incensed him.

"I don't expect to try!" she retorted blithely. "I don't see that I'd gain anything, if I *did* understand. You and Elizabeth are a great deal too —"

He interrupted overbearingly: —

"Leave Elizabeth out! Confine your remarks to me!"

"My remarks will be wholly unconfined," said Elsie, as she trotted forward.

He scrambled alongside in silent rage. Perhaps he was thinking of his inability to reach protected female license. He may obscurely have felt that life's department of justice was being balked at the moment by its department of natural history —a not uncommon interference in this too crowded world. At least he put himself on record about it: —

"If you were a boy, Elsie, you'd get taken down a buttonhole!"

"Don't you worry about my buttonholes!" chirped Elsie. "My buttonholes are where they ought to be!"

It was not the first time that he had made something of this sort for Elizabeth. One morning of the May preceding he had pulled apart the boughs of a blooming lilac bush in the yard, and had seen a nest with four pale-green eggs. That autumn during a ramble in the woods and fields he had taken burrs and made a nest and deposited in it four pale-green half-ripe horse chestnuts.

Elizabeth, who did not amount to much in this world but breath and a soft cloud of hair and sentiment, had loyally carried it off to her cabinet of nests. These were duly arranged on shelves, and labelled according to species and life and love: "The Meadow Lark's" —"The Blue-bird's" —"The Orchard Oriole's" —"The Brown Thrasher's"; on and on along the shelves. At the end of a row she placed this treasured curiosity, and inscribed it, "An Imitation by a Young Animal."

Elizabeth's humor was a mild beam.

Do country children in that part of the world make such playthings now? Do they still look to wild life and not wholly to the shops of cities for the satisfying of their instincts for toys and games and fancies?

Do alder stalks still race down dusty country lanes as thoroughbred colts, afterwards to be tied in their stalls in fence corners with halters of green hemp? Does any little rustic instrument-maker now draw melodies from a homegrown corn-stalk? Across rattling window-panes of old farm-houses —between withered sashes-during long winter nights does there sound the æolian harp made with a hair from a horse-tail? Do boys still squeeze the red juice of poke-berries on the plumage of white barnyard roosters, thus whenever they wish bringing on a cock-fight between old far-squandered Cochins, who long previously had entered into a treaty as to their spheres of influence in a Manchuria of hens? Do the older boys some wet night lead the youngest around the corner of the house in the darkness and show him, there! rising out of the ground! the long expected Devil come at last (as a pumpkin carved and candle-lighted) for his own particular urchin? When in autumn the great annual ceremony of the slaughter of the swine takes place on the farms at the approach of the winter solstice, —a festival running back to aboriginal German tribes before the beginnings of agriculture, when the stock that had been fattened on the mast and pasturage of the mountains was driven down into the villages and perforce killed to keep it from starving, —when this carnival of flesh recurs on Kentucky farms, do boys with turkey-quills or goose-quills blow the bladders up, tie the necks and hang them in smoke-houses or garrets to dry; and then at daybreak of Christmas morning, having warmed and expanded them before the fire, do they jump on them and explode them —a primitive folk-rite for making a magnificent noise ages older than the use of crackers and cannon?

Do children contrive their picture-frames by glueing October acorns and pine-cones to ovals of boards and giving the mass a thick coat of varnish? On winter nights do little girls count the seeds of the apples they are eating and pronounce over them the incantation of their destinies-thus in another guise going through the same charm of words that Marguerite used as she scattered earthward the petals of trust and ruin? Do they, sitting face to face bareheaded on sun-hued meadows, pluck the dandelion when its seed are clustered at the top like a ball of gauze, and with one breath try to blow these off: for the number of seed that remain will tell the too many years before they shall be asked in marriage? Do they slit the stems and cast them into the near brook and watch them form into ringlets and floating hair-as of a water spirit? Do they hold buttercups under each other's chins to see who likes butter-that is, mind you, *good* butter! Romping little Juliets of Nature's proud courtyards-with young Montagues watching from afar! Sane little Ophelias of the garland at the water's brink-secure for many years yet from all sad Hamlets! Do country children do such things and have such notions now?

Perhaps once in a lifetime, on some summer day when the sky was filled with effulgence and white clouds, you may have seen a large low-flying bird cross the landscape straight away from you, so exactly poised under the edge of a cloud, that one of the wings beat in shadow while the other waved in light. Thus these two children, following their path over the fields that morning, ran along the dividing-line between the darkness and the light of their world.

On one side of them lay the thinning shadow of man's ancient romance with Nature which is everywhere most rapidly dying out in this civilization-the shadow of that romance which for ages was the earliest ray of his religion: in later centuries became the splendor of his art; then loomed as the historic background of his titanic myths and fables; and now only in obscure valleys is found lingering in the play of superstitious children at twilights before darkness engulfs them-the latest of the infants in the dusk of the oldest gods.

On the other side blazed the hard clear light of that realism of human life which is the unfolding brightness of the New World; that light of reason and of reasonableness which seems to take from man both his mornings and his evenings, with all their half-lights and their mysteries; and to leave him only a perpetual noonday of the actual in which everything loses its shadow. So the two ran that morning. But so children ever run-between the fresh light and the old darkness of ever-advancing humanity-between the world's new birth and a forgetting.

On the brother and sister skipped and bounded, wild with health and Christmas joy. Their quarrel was in a moment forgotten-happy children! The nature of the little girl was not deep enough to remember a quarrel; the boy's nature was too deep to remember one. Crimson-tipped, madcap, winter spirits! The blue dome vaulting infinitely above them with all its clouds pushed aside; the wind throwing itself upon them at every step like some huge young animal force unchained for exercise and rude in its good-natured play. As they crossed a woodland pasture the hoary trees rocked and roared, strewing in their path bits of bark and rotten twigs and shattered sprigs of mistletoe. In an open meadow a yellow-breasted lark sprang reluctantly from its cuddling-place and drifted far behind them on the rushing air. In a corn-field out of a dried bunch of partridge grass a rabbit started softly and went bobbing away over the corn-rows —with its white flag run up at the rear end of the fortifications as a notice "Please not to shoot or otherwise trespass!" Alas, that so palpable and polite a request should be treated as so plain a target!

Once the little girl changed her trotting gait to a walk nearly as fast, so that her skirts swished from side to side of her plump hips with wren-like energy and briskness. Her mind was still harping on her father; and having satirized him, and adoring him, she now would fain approve him.

"My! but it's cold, Herbert! Papa says it is not sickness that plays havoc with you: it's not being ready for sickness; and being ready depends upon how you have lived: it depends upon what you are; and that's where your virtue comes in, my child, if you have any virtue. We have been taught to stay out of doors when it is cold; and now we can come out when it is colder. We were ready for the crisis!" and Elsie pushed her nose into the air with smallish amusement.

The boy gravely pondered her words about crisis, and pondered his own before replying: —

"I wonder what kind of children we'd have been if we'd had some other father. Or some other *mother*," he added with a change of tone as he uttered that last word; and he looked askance at his sister to see whether she would glance at him.

She kept her face set straight forward; but she impatiently exclaimed: —

"Others, others, others! You are always thinking of *others*, Herbert!"

"I am one of them myself! I am one of the others myself!" cried the boy, relieved that his secret was his own; and bounding suddenly on the earth also as if with a sense of his kinship to its unseen host.

The question he had asked marked him: for he was one of the children who from the outset begin to ask of life what it means and who are surprised when there is no one to tell them. For him there was no rest until he solved some mystery or had at least found out where some mystery stood abandoned on the road —a mystery still. Her intelligence stopped short at what she perfectly knew. She saw with amazing clearness, but she beheld very little. Hers was that order of intelligence which is gifted with vision of almost terrifying accuracy-at short range: life is a thin painted curtain, and its depths are the painted curtain's depths.

Once they came to a pair of bars which led into a meadow. The bars were of green timber and were very heavy. As he strained and tugged at them, she waited close behind him, dancing to the right and to the left so that there was a sound of mud-crystals being crushed under her tyrannical little fat feet.

"Hurry, hurry, hurry!" she exclaimed with impatience. "We may run in the cold, but we must not stand still in the cold;" and she kicked him on the heels and pummelled him between the shoulders with her muff.

"I am doing my best," he said, laughing heartily.

"Your best is not good enough," she urged, laughing heartily likewise.

"This bar is wedged tight. It's the sap that's frozen to the post. Look out there behind!"

He stepped back, and, with a short run, lifted his leg and kicked the bar with his full strength. The recoil threw him backward to the ground, but he was quickly on his feet again; and as the bar was now loosened, he let it down for her. She stepped serenely through and without looking back or waiting trotted on. He put the bars up and with a spurt soon overtook her, for the meadow they were now crossing had been closely grazed in the autumn and there was better walking. They went up rising ground and reached one of those dome-like elevations which are a feature of the blue-grass country.

Straight ahead of them half a mile away stood the house toward which they were hastening; a two-story brick house, lifted a little above its surroundings of yard and gardens and shrubbery and vines: an oak-tree over its roof, cedar-trees near its windows, ivy covering one of its walls, a lawn sloping from it to a thicket of evergreens where its Christmas Tree each year was cut.

The children greeted with fresh enthusiasm the sight of this charming, this ideal place to which they were transferring their Christmas plans and pleasures-abandoning their own hearth-stone. There lived their father's friend; there lived Harold and Elizabeth, their friends; and there lived the wife and mother of the household-the woman toward whom from their infancy they had been herded as by a driving hand.

The tell-tale Christmas smoke of the land was pouring from its chimneys, showing that it was being warmed through and through for coming guests and coming festivities. At one end of the building, in an ell, was the kitchen; it sent forth a volume of smoke, the hospitable invitations of which there was no misunderstanding. At the opposite end was the parlor: it stood for the Spirit, as the kitchen for the honest Flesh: the wee travellers on the distant hilltop thought of the flesh first.

They had no idea of the origin of the American Christmas. They did not know that this vast rolling festival has migrated to the New World, drawing with it things gathered from many lands and centuries; that the cooking and the feasting crossed from pagan England; that the evergreen with its lights and gifts came from pagan Germany; that the mystical fireside with its stockings was introduced from Holland; that the evergreen now awaiting them in the shut and darkened parlor of this Kentucky farm-house represented the sacred Tree which has been found in nearly every ancient land and is older than the Tree of Life in the literature of Eden.

As far as they thought of the antiquity of the Christmas festival at all, it had descended straight from the Holy Land and the Manger of Bethlehem; this error now led to complications.

The boy's crimson skull-cap had a peak which curled forward; and attached to this peak by several inches of crewel hung a round crimson ball about the size of the seed-ball of a sycamore. The shifting wind blew it hither and thither so that it buffeted him in the face and eyes. On this exposed height, especially, the wind raced free; and he ducked his head and turned his face sidewise toward her-an imp of winter joy-as he shouted across the gale: —

"If people are still baking such quantities of cake in memory of Christmas after all these hundreds of years, don't you suppose, Elsie, that the Apostles must have been fearful cake-eaters? To have left such an impression on the world! Cake *is* a kind of sacred thing at home even yet, isn't it? A fine cake looks still as if it was baked for an Apostle! Doesn't it? Now doesn't it?"

Elsie did not reply at once. Her younger brother was growing into the habit of saying unex-pected things. Once after he had left the breakfast table, she had heard her father say to her mother that he had genius. Elsie was not positive as to all that genius comprised; but she at once decided that if she did not possess genius she did not wish genius. However she packed herself off to her room and thought further about this unpleasant parental discrimination.

"If he has genius," she said finally, "at least he did not get it from *them*," and there was a triumph in her eye. "I see not the slightest sign of genius in either of *them*: he must have gotten it from our grandparents-never from *them*!"

From that moment she had begun to oppose her mind to his mind as a superior working instrument in a practical world. Whenever he put forth a fancy, she put forth a fact; and the fact was meant to extinguish the fancy as a muffler puts out a candle. After a moment she now replied-with a mind that had repudiated genius: —

"Nothing is said in the New Testament, my child, about cake. The only thing mentioned is loaves and fishes. But they *do* seem to have done an unconscionable amount of dining on bread and fish!" and Elsie had her own satirical laugh at the table customs of ancient Palestine as viewed from the Kentucky standard of the nineteenth century.

The boy before replying deliberated as always.

"They may not have had cake, but they had meat: because they said he sat with sinners at meat. I wonder why it was always *the sinners* who got *the meat*!"

Elsie could offer no personal objection to this: Providence had ordained her to dwell in the tents of flesh herself.

"How could they feed five thousand people on five loaves and two fishes? How *could* they? At one of those fish dinners!"

"They did it!" said Elsie flatly. She saw the whole transaction with brilliant clearness-saw to the depths of the painted curtain. It was as naturally fact as the family four of them at breakfast that morning, fed on home-smoked sausages and perfectly digestible buckwheat cakes.

"And twelve baskets of crumbs! That makes it worse! With bread for thousands everywhere, why pick up crumbs?"

"Nothing is said about crumbs; they were fragments."

"But if I've got to believe it, I've got to think how they did it! I've *got* to! If I can't think of it as it is, I must think of it as it isn't! But I can't do anything with the loaves; I give up the bread. However, I think those two fish might have been leviathans. That would be only two thousand five hundred people to each leviathan. Many of them might not have liked leviathan. I wouldn't have wanted any! They could have skipped me! They could have had my slice! And the babies-they didn't want *much*! Anyhow, that's the best I can do for the fish"; and he had his laugh also-not an incessant ripple like hers, but a music issuing from the depths of him through joy in the things he saw.

Elsie made the reply which of late was becoming habitual in her talks with him.

"Don't begin to be *peculiar*, Herbert. You are too young to be *peculiar*. Leave that to old people!" and Elsie's mind glided off from the loaves and the fishes of Galilee to certain old people of her neighborhood from whose eccentricities she extracted acrid amusement.

The boy's words were not irreverent; irreverence had never been taught him; he did not know what irreverence was. They merely expressed the primary action of his mind in dealing with what to him was a wonder-story of Nature. And yet with this same mind which asked of wonder that it be reasonable, he was on his way to the celebration of Christmas Eve and to the story of the Nativity-the most joyous, the most sad, the most sublime Nature-story of mankind.

His unconscious requirement was that this also must be reasonable; if it were not, he would accept the portions that were reasonable and reject the others as now too childish for his fore-handed American brain.

They were nearing the end of their bitter walk. The little girl as she hurried forward now and then strained her eyes toward the opposite ends of the house ahead; at the kitchen smoke which promised such gifts to the flesh; at the window-shutters of the darkened parlor where the Christmas Tree stood, soon to be decorated with presents: some for her-the little fat mercenary now approaching who was positive that during these days of preparation she had struck a shrewd bargain with the Immortal.

The boy, too, looked at these windows; but especially he looked at another between them, from which perhaps Elizabeth was watching for him.

Once he turned, and, walking backward, directed his gaze from this high point far across the country. Somewhere back there his father might now be stopping at a farm-house. A malignant disease was raging among the children of the neighborhood, some of whom were his schoolmates and friends; the holidays would bring no merry Christmas for them.

Wherever his father might be, there an influence started and came rushing across the landscape like the shadow of a cloud. It fell upon him, and travelled on toward the house he was approaching; it disappeared within the house and fell upon the woman who so wonderfully moved about in it: a chilling mysterious shadow that bound the three of them-his father and himself and this gentle woman-together in a band of darkness.

Then he faced about and ran on, longing the more ardently for Elizabeth: the path between him and Elizabeth lay before his nimble feet like a band of light.

II. When a Boy Finds Out About His Father

On the day preceding that twenty-fourth of December when his two weather-proof untrammelled children were rioting over the frozen earth, Dr. Birney met with an event which may here be set down as casting the first direct light upon him. Some reflected radiance may already have gone glancing in his direction from the luminous prattle of his offspring; some obscure glimpses must therein have bodied him forth: and the portraits that children unconsciously paint of people-what trained hand ever drew such living lines?

A short stretch across the country from his comfortable manor house there towered in stateliness one of the finest homesteads of this region; and in the great bedroom of this house, in the mother's bed, there had lain for days one of his patients critically ill, the only child of an intense mother who was herself no longer young.

Early that morning upon setting out he had driven rapidly to this house, gotten quickly out, and been quickly received through the front door thrown open to admit him. After examining the child, he had turned to the mother and spoken the words that are probably the happiest ever to fall from any tongue upon any ear: —

"He is out of danger. He is getting well."

At this intelligence the mother forgot the presence of another mother older than herself who had come to be with her during these vigils and anxieties. As the doctor, having spoken a few words to the nurse, passed out into the hall toward the hat-rack, she led him into the parlors; she pulled him down into a chair beside the one she took; she caught his hand in hers and drew it into her lap. She forgot that after all she was a woman and he was a man; she remembered only that she was a mother and he a physician; and unnerved by the relief from days and nights of tension, she poured out her quivering gratitude.

The doctor with a warm light in his eyes listened; and he was flushed with pleasure also at his skill in bringing his case through; but she had scarcely begun before his expression showed embarrassment. Gratitude rendered him ill at ease: who can thank Science? Who can thank a man for doing his duty and his best? With a smile of deprecation he interrupted: —

"A great surgeon of France centuries ago was accustomed to say of a convalescent patient: 'God cured him; I dressed him.' I do not know whether, if I dared speak for the science of medicine near the close of the nineteenth century, I could say that. That is not the language of science now. If science thanks anything, it thanks other sciences and respects itself. But I will say that I might not have been able to save the life of your son if he had not been a healthy child-and a happy one; for happiness in a child is of course one of its signs of health. In his case I did not have to treat a patient with a disease; I had merely to treat a disease in a patient: and there is a great difference. The patient kept out of the case altogether, or in so far as he entered it, he entered it as my assistant. But if he had not been healthy and happy, the result might have been-well, different."

The mother's face became more radiant.

"If his health and happiness helped him through," she exclaimed, "then his mother enters into the case; for his health was his birthright from his parents; and his happiness-on account of the absence of his father during most of his life when he has been awake-has been a gift from his mother. He has lived with Happiness; Happiness has been before his eyes; Happiness has filled his ears; Happiness has held him in its arms; Happiness has danced for his feet; Happiness has rocked him to sleep; Happiness has smiled over him when he awoke. He has not known anything but Happiness because Happiness has been his mother. And so, if he owes the preservation of his life to Happiness, he owes it to the instinct of maternal imitation."

The doctor had heard this carolling of maternity with full approval-this heaven-rising skylark song of motherhood; but at the last sentence he pricked up his ears with disfavor and stopped smiling: with him these were marks that he had withdrawn his intellectual fellowship. The trouble was that he esteemed her a charming and irreproachable woman and wife and mother; but that he could accord her no rank as a scientist, no standing whatsoever; and therefore he must part company with her when she spoke for instincts. The instinct of maternal imitation-the vanity of it! That her sex could believe a child to be sent into this world by the great Mother of all wisdom and given so poor a start as to be placed under the tyranny of an instinct to imitate any other imperfect human being-man or woman.

Perhaps it was one of his weaknesses, when he came upon a case of folly, to wish to perform an operation in mental surgery at once-and without anæsthetics, in order that the wide-awake intelligence of the sufferer might be enlisted against the recurrence of such a necessity.

In a tone of affectionate forbearance he now said: —

"If only there were any such thing in Nature as the instinct of maternal imitation! Children have enough instincts to battle with and fight their way through, as it is. Let me beg of you not to teach your child anything as criminally wrong as that; and don't you be so criminally wrong as to believe it!"

The mother's countenance fell. She released the doctor's hand and pushed her chair back; and she brushed out her lap with both hands as though his words might somehow have fallen into it, and she did not wish them to remain there. She spoke caustically: —

"No intimate sacred bond between mother and child which guides it to imitate her?"

She felt as though he had attacked the very citadel of motherhood; as though he had over-thrown the tested and adopted standards of universal thinking, the very basic idea of existence; and she recoiled from this as a taint of eccentricity in him-that early death-knell of a physician's usefulness.

But the doctor swept her words away with gay warmth: —

"Oh, there is the intimate sacred bond, of course! No doubt the most intimate, the most sacred in this world. Believe in that all you can: the more the better! But we are not speaking of that: that has nothing to do with this imagined instinct of maternal imitation. Don't you know that a foundling in a foundling asylum as instinctively imitates its nurse? Don't you know that a child as instinctively imitates its stepmother-if it loves her? Don't you know that a child as instinctively imitates its grandmother?"

The mother lay back in her chair and looked at him without a word. But then, Doctor Birney could be rude, curt, brutal. In proof of which he now leaned over toward her and continued with more gentleness: —

"Do you not know that every child in this world begins its advance into life by one path only-the path of least resistance? and its path of least resistance is paved and lined with what it likes! As soon as it can do anything for itself, it tries to do what it likes, and it never tries to do anything else. When, later on, a time comes when it can be persuaded to do a thing that it has already desired *not* to do, then its will comes into the case; it ceases to be simply a little animal and becomes a little human animal; it begins to be moral and heroic instead of unmoral and unheroic. But we are not talking about that. The best we can do is to call those earliest movements of its life the reaching out of its instincts and its taking hold of things that are like its own leading traits. The parallel is in Nature where the tendril of a vine takes hold of the matured branch of the same vine and pulls itself up by this. Thus one generation knits itself to another through the binding of like to like; and that is the whole bond between mother and child or father and child: it is like attaching itself to like under the influence of love. In this world every subject has two doors: you open one, and the good things come out. You open the other, and the evil things come out. This subject has its two doors: and I open first the door of Mother of Pearl-for you two pearls of mothers! Out of it come all the exquisite radiant traits that bind mothers and children. How many great men in history have begun their growth by attaching themselves to the great traits of their mothers? Then there is the other door. I am sorry to open it, but whether I open it or not, opened it will be: the Door of Ebony behind which are imprisoned all the dark things that bind parents and children. I am afraid I shall have to illustrate: if a child is born mendacious and its mother has mendacity as one of her leading traits, its little mendacity will flourish on her large mendacity. If it is born deceitful, and hypocrisy is one of her traits, hypocrisy in it will pull itself up by taking hold of hypocrisy in her. If it is born quick-tempered, and if ungovernable temper is one of her failings, every exhibition of this in her will foster its impatience and lack of self-control. These are some few of the dreadful things that come out: and if it is dreadful even to speak of them, think how much more dreadful to see them alive and to set them at work! Now let's shut the dark Door! And let us hope that some day Nature herself may not be able to open it ever again!"

Hitherto the older of the two mothers, the mother of many children, had remained silent with that peculiar expression of patience and sweetness which lies like a halo on the faces of good women who have brought many children into the world. She now spoke as if to release many thoughts weighing heavily upon her.

"It has always been my trouble-not that my children would not imitate me, but that they *would* imitate me! I have my faults, for I am human; and I can endure them as long as they remain mine. They have ceased to give me much concern. I suppose in a way I have grown attached to them, just as I like people whom I do not entirely approve. But as soon as I see the children reproducing my faults, these become responsibilities. They keep me awake at night; sometimes they distress me almost beyond endurance. I know I have spent many anxious years with this problem. And I know also that the only times when their father has been overanxious about his failings has been when the boys have imitated *him*. He is always ready to lead a splendid attack on his faults, and they march at him from the direction of the boys!"

"And so," said the doctor, laughing, "this instinct of parental imitation is an instrument safe to take by the handle, and dangerous to grasp by the blade!"

He knew fathers in the neighborhood who were dreading the time when their sons might begin to imitate them-too far. And other fathers dreading the hour when their sons might cease to imitate their sires, and wander away preferably to imitate persons outside the family connection, —possibly an instinct of non-parental imitation!

He rose to go in a mood of great good nature, and looked from one to the other of the two mothers: —

"Perhaps Nature protected children from the danger of imitating by not making it their duty to imitate. And perhaps, as all parents are imperfect human beings, she may have thought it simple justice to children to confer upon them the right to be disobedient. At least, if there is an instinct to obey, it is backed up with an equal instinct not to obey; and the two seem to have been left to fight it out between themselves; and that perhaps is the great battle-field where incessant fighting goes on between parents and children. And at least disobedience has been of equal value with obedience in the making of human history, in the development of the race. For if children had simply obeyed their parents, if the young had been born merely to ape the old, there never would have been any human young and old. We should all still be apes, even if we had developed as far as that. You two ladies-of course with greatly modified features-might be throwing cocoanuts at each other on the tops of two rival palm-trees. Or-as the dutiful daughters of dutiful mothers-you might be taking afternoon naps in an oasis of dates-all because of that instinct of maternal imitation!"

He hurried out to the hat-rack, making his retreat at the top of his own high spirits, they following; and with one glove on he held out his hand to the mother of the sick boy: —

"I'll come in the morning to see how he is-and to see how his mother is. Now shake hands and say I have been a good doctor to you both."

The mother's reply showed that bitterness rankled in her, as she yielded her hand coldly: —

"Even if you have tried to destroy for me the intimate sacred bond between a mother and her child, I don't think you will be able to deny that my boy is a healthy and happy child because he is a child of a perfect marriage!" And she looked with secret and shaded import at the other mother.

As the doctor drove out of the yard her last words lingered —*the healthy children of a perfect marriage.* And the look the two mothers had exchanged! It was as though each had a sword in her eye and touched him with the point of it-hinting that he merited being run through.

How often during these years he had encountered that same look from other mothers of the neighborhood!

"But if a wound like that could have been fatal," he reflected, "if a wound like that could have finished me, I should not have been here to save the life of her boy; he would have been dead this morning."

Then his mind under the rigor of long training passed to happier subjects. His success in the case of this child was one more triumph in his long list; it renewed his grip on power within him.

But for the necessity to provide for a people the services of general practitioner, Dr. Birney would have made a specialty of children's diseases. The happiest moment he experienced in his profession was a day such as this when he could announce the triumph of his skill and the saving of a young life. There was no sadder one than any day on which he walked out of the sick chamber and at the threshold met the gaunt ancient Presence, waiting to stalk in and take the final charge of the case given up by the vanquished physician. And when a few days later he sat in his buggy on the turnpike at the end of a procession-his healthy little patient stretched prostrate at the other end-he driving there as the public representative of a science that was ages old and that had gathered from all lands the wisdom of the best minds but was still impotent-on such a day he went down to his lowest defeat.

He had such faith in the future of his science that he looked forward to the time when there would be no such monstrous tragedy on this planet as infant mortality. No healthy child would ever be allowed to die of disease; disease would never be permitted to reach it, or reaching it, would be arrested as it arrived. The vast multitude of physicians and surgeons now camped around the morning of life, waiting to receive the incoming generations on the rosy mountain-tops of its dawn-nearly all these would be withdrawn; they would move across the landscape of the world and pitch their tents on the plains of waning daylight; there to receive the ragged and broken army that came staggering from the battle-field, every soldier more or less wounded, every soldier more or less weary; there to give them a twilight of least suffering, their sundown of peace; and there to arrange that the great dark Gates closed on them softly.

The conversation that morning disclosed among other facts the secret dread of Dr. Birney's life: that the time would come when his children, especially his boy, might begin to imitate him more than he desired. For a long time now he had kept under closest observation the working out in each of them of the law of like attaching itself to like; for already this had borne fruit for both on the vine of his own profession.

A physician in a city may practise his profession with complete segregation from the members of his family; his office may be miles away; if he sees his patients in his house, his children are kept in another part of it. But out in the country the whole house is open; the children rove everywhere; if their father is a physician, they know when he starts and when he returns; and there is displayed in full view the entire drama of his life. And this life is twofold: for the physician must demonstrate as no member of any other profession is required to do-that whoever would best serve mankind must first best serve himself. In this service he must reach a solution of the selfish and the unselfish; he must reconcile the world's two warring philosophies of egoism and altruism. The outside world has its attention fixed solely upon the drama of the physician's public service to it; for the members of his own family is reserved acquaintance with the drama of his devotion to himself. Well for him and well for them if they do not misunderstand!

Each of Dr. Birney's children responded to the attraction of a phase of his life-the phase that appealed to a leading trait in each.

From the time of the little girl's beginning to observe her father she was influenced by what looked to her like his self-love: his care about what he ate and drank; his changing of his clothes whenever he came home, whether they were drenched or were dry; his constant washing of his hands; all this pageant of self-adulation mirrored itself in her consciousness. When he was away from home, she could still follow him by her mother's solicitude for his comfort and safety. To

Elsie's mother the ill were not so much a source of anxiety as a husband who was perfectly well; and thus there had been built up in Elsie herself the domineering idea that her father was the all-important personage in the neighborhood as a consequence of thinking chiefly of himself. Selfishness in her reached out and twined itself like a tendril about selfishness in him; and she proceeded to lift herself up and grow by this vital bond.

Too young to transmit this resemblance, she did what she could to pass it on to the next generation: she handed it down and disseminated it in her doll-house. There was something terrifying and grim and awful in the fatalistic accuracy with which Elsie reproduced her father's selfishness among her dolls, because it was on a mimic scale what is going on all over the world: the weaving by children's fingers of parental designs long perpetuated in the tapestry of Nature; the same old looms, the same old threads, the same old designs-but new fingers.

One of the dolls was known as "the doctor"; the others were the members of his family and his domestics. This puppet was a perfect child-image of the god of self-idolatry, as set up in the person of a certain Dr. Downs Birney, and as observed by his very loyal and most affectionate and highly amused daughter Elsie.

One day the doctor, quietly passing the opened door of the nursery, saw Elsie on the floor with her back turned to him faithfully copying and dramatizing some of the daily scenes of his professional life. His eyes shone with humor as he looked on; but there was sadness in them as he turned silently away.

With the boy it was otherwise. The earliest notion of his father the boy had grasped was that of always travelling toward the sick-to a world that needed him. All the roads of the neighborhood-turnpikes, lanes, carriage-tracks, wagon-tracks, foot-paths —met at his father's house; if you followed any one of them long enough, sooner or later you would reach some one who was sick.

When he was quite young his father began to take him in his buggy on his circuits; and at every house where they stopped, he witnessed this never-ending drama of need and aid. Such countenances people had as they followed his father out to the buggy where he was holding the reins! Such happy faces-or so sad, so sad! Souls hanging on his father's word as though life went on with it or went to pieces with it. Actually his father had no business of his own: he merely drove about and enabled other people to attend to their business! He one day asked him why he did not *sometimes* do something for himself and the family!

Thus a leading trait in him gripped that branch of his father's life where hung his service to others; and by this vital bond it lifted itself up and began to flourish in its long travel toward maturity. He literally took hold of his father, as a social implement, by the well-worn handle of common use.

His presence in the buggy with his father was not incidental; it was the doctor's design. He wished to have the boy along during these formative years in order that he might get the right start toward the great things of life as these one by one begin to break in upon the attention of a growing boy. The doctor wanted to be the first to talk with him-the first to sow the right suggestions: it was one of his sayings that the earliest suggestions rooted in the mind of the child will be the final things to drop from the dying man's brain: what goes in first comes out last.

And so there began to be many conversations; incredible questions; answers not always forthcoming. And a series of revelations ensued; the boy revealing his growth to a watchful father, and a father revealing his life to a very watchful son! These revelations began to look like mile-stones on life's road, marked with further understandings.

Thus, one day when the boy was a good deal younger than now, his father had come home and had gotten ready to go away again and was sitting before the fire, looking gravely into it and taking solitary counsel about some desperate case, as the country doctor must often do. Being a very little fellow then, he had straddled one of his father's mighty legs and had balanced himself by resting his hands on his father's mighty shoulders.

"Is somebody very sick?"

The head under the weather-roughened hat nodded silently.

"I wonder how it happens that all the sick are in our neighborhood."

A smile flitted across the doctor's mouth.

"The sick are in all neighborhoods, little wonderer."

He said this cheerfully. It was his idea-and he tried to enforce it at home-that young children must never, if possible, make the acquaintance of the words *bad* and *sad* —nor of the realities that are masked behind them. He especially believed that what the old are familiar with as life's tragic laws ought never to be told to children as tragic: what is inevitable should never be presented to them as misfortunes.

Therefore he now declared that the sick are in all neighborhoods as he might have stated that there are wings on all birds, or leaves on all growing apple trees.

"Not all over the world?" asked the boy, enlarging his vision in space.

"All over the world," admitted the doctor with entire cheerfulness; the fact was a matter of no consequence.

"Not all the time?" asked the boy, enlarging his outlook in time.

"All the time! All over the world and all the time!" conceded the doctor, as though this made not the slightest difference to a human being.

"Isn't there a single minute when everybody is well everywhere?"

"Not a single, solitary minute."

"Then somebody must always be suffering."

The doctor nodded again; the matter was not worth speaking of.

"Then somebody else must always be sorry."

The doctor bowed encouragingly.

"Then I am sorry, too!"

This time the doctor did not move his head, and he did not open his lips. He saw that a new moment had arrived in the boy's growth —a consciousness of the universal tragedy and personal share and sorrow in it. He knew that many people never feel this; some feel it late; a few feel it early; he had always said that children should never feel it. He knew also that when once it has begun, it never ends. Nothing ever banishes it or stills it-that perception of the human tragedy and one's share and sorrow in it.

He did not welcome its appearance now, in his son least of all. For an instant he charged himself with having made a mistake in taking the child along on his visits to the sick, thus making known too early the dark side of happy neighborhood life. Then he went further back and traced this premature seriousness to its home and its beginning: in prenatal depression-in a mother's anguish and a wife's despair. It was a bitter retrospect: it kept him brooding.

The chatter was persistent. A hand was stretched up, and it took hold of his chin and shook it: —

"There ought to be a country where nobody suffers and there ought to be a time; a large country and a long time."

"There is such a country and there is such a time, Herbert," said the doctor, now with some sadness.

"Then I'll warrant you it's part of the United States," cried the boy, getting his idea of mortality slightly mixed with his early Americanism. "Texas would hold them, wouldn't it? Don't you think Texas could contain them all and contain them forever?"

The doctor laughed and seemed to think enough had been said on the subject of large enough graveyards for the race.

"Why don't you doctors send your patients to that country?"

"Perhaps we do sometimes!" The doctor laughed again.

"Do you ever send yours?"

"Possibly."

"And how many do you send?"

"I don't know!" exclaimed the doctor, laughing this time without being wholly amused. "I don't know, and I never intend to try to find out."

"When I grow up we'll practise together and send twice as many," the boy said, looking into his father's eyes with the flattery of professional imitation.

"So we will! There'll be no trouble about that! Twice as many, perhaps three times! No trouble whatever!"

He took the hands from his shoulders and laid them in the palm of his and studied them—those masculine boyish hands that had never touched any of the world's suffering. And then he looked at his own hands which had handled so much of the world's suffering, but had never reached happiness; happiness which for years had dwelt just at his finger-tips but beyond arm's reach.

Not very long afterwards another conversation lettered another mile-stone in the progress of mutual understanding.

It was a beautiful drowsy May morning near noon, and the two were driving slowly homeward along the turnpike. When the lazily trotting horse reached the front gate of a certain homestead, he stopped and threw one ear backward as a living interrogation point. As his answer, he got an unexpected cut in the flank with the tip of the lash that was like the sting of a hornet: a reminder that the driver was not alone in the buggy; that the horse should have known he was not alone; and that what he did when alone was a matter of confidence between master and beast.

The boy, who had been thrown backward, heels high, laughed as he settled himself again on his cushion: —

"He thought you wanted to turn in."

"He thinks too much-sometimes."

"Don't they ever get sick there?"

"I suppose they do."

"*Then* you turn in!"

"Then I *don't* turn in."

"Aren't you their doctor?"

"I was the doctor once."

"Where was I?"

"I don't know where you were; you were not born."

"So many things happened before I was born; I wish they hadn't!"

"It is a pity; I had the same experience."

The buggy rolled slowly along homeward. On one side of the road were fields of young Indian corn, the swordlike blades flashing in the sun; on the other side fields of red clover blooming; the fragrance was wafted over the fence to the buggy. Further, in a soft grassy lawn, on a little knoll shaded by a white ash, a group of sleek cattle stood content in their blameless world. Over the prostrate cows one lordly head, its incurved horns deep hidden by its curls, kept guard. The scene was a living Kentucky replica of Paul Potter's *Bull*.

"Drive!" murmured the doctor, handing over the reins; and he drew his hat low over his eyes and set his shoulder against his corner of the buggy; he often caught up with sleep while on the road. And he often tried to catch up with thinking.

The horse always knew when the reins changed hands. He disregarded the proxy, kept his own gait, picked the best of the road, and turned out for passing vehicles. The boy now grasped the lines with unexpected positiveness; and he leaned over and looked up under the rim of his father's hat: —

"I hope the doctor they employ will give them the wrong medicines," he confided. "I hope the last one of them will have many a rattling good bellyache for their meanness to you!"

Then more years for father and son, each finding the other out.

And now finally on the morning of that twenty-fourth day of December, the father was to witness a scene in the drama of his life as amazingly performed by his son-illustrating what a little actor can do when he undertakes to imitate an old actor to whom he is most loyal.

That morning after breakfast the apt pupil in Life's School had been sent for, and when he had entered the library, his father was sitting before the fire, idle. The buggy was not waiting outside; the hat and overcoat and gloves were nowhere in sight; and he had not gotten ready his satchel which took the place of the saddlebags of earlier generations when the country doctor travelled around on horseback and carried the honey of physic packed at his thighs-like a wingless, befattened bumblebee. This morning it looked as though all the sick were well at last; it was a sound if wicked world; and nothing was left for a physician but to be happy in it-without a profession-and without wickedness.

He threw himself into his father's impulsively opened arms, and was heaved high into his lap. Though he was growing rather mature for laps now; he was beginning to speculate about having something of a lap of his own; quite a good deal of a lap.

"How is the children's epidemic to-day?"

"Never you mind about the children's epidemic! I'll take care of the children's epidemic," repeated the doctor, pulling the long-faced, autumn-faced prodigy of all questions between his knees and looking him over with secret solicitude. "We'll not talk about sick children, but about two well children-thanked be the Father of all children! So you and Elsie are going away to help celebrate a Christmas Tree."

"Yes; but when are you going to have a Christmas Tree of our own?"

Now, that subject had two prongs, and the doctor seized the prong that did not pierce family affairs-did not pierce *him*. He settled down to the subject with splendid warmth and heartiness: —

"Well, let me see! You may have your first Christmas Tree as soon as you are old enough to commence to do things for other people; as soon as you can receive into your head the smallest hard pill of an idea about your duty to millions and millions and millions of your fellow medicine takers. Can you understand that?"

"Gracious! That would be a *big* pill-larger than my head! I don't see what it has to do with one miserable little dead pine tree!"

The doctor roared.

"It has this to do with one miserable dead pine tree: don't you know yet that Christmas Trees are in memory of a boy who was once exactly your age and height-and perhaps with your appetite-and with just as many eyes and possibly even more questions? The boy grew up to be a man. The man became a teacher. The teacher became a neighborhood doctor. The neighborhood doctor became the greatest physician of the world-and he never took a fee!"

"Ah, yes! But he wasn't a better doctor than *you* are, was he? If he'd come into this neighborhood and tried to practise, you'd soon have ousted him, wouldn't you, with your doses and soups and jellies?"

"Humph!" grunted the doctor with a wry twist of the mouth; "I suppose I would! Yes; undoubtedly I'd have ousted him! He could never have competed with me in *my* practice; never! But we won't try that hard little pill of an idea any more. We'll drop the subject of Christmas Trees for one more year. Perhaps by that time you can take the pill as a powder! So! I hear you are going to attend a dancing party; we'll talk about the party. And you are going over there to stay all night. I wish I were going. I wish I were going over there to stay all night," reiterated the man, with an outrush of solemn tenderness that reached back through vain years, through so many parched, unfilled years.

"I wish so, too," cried the boy, instantly burying his face on his father's coat-sleeve, then lifting it again and looking at him with a guilty flush which the doctor did not observe.

"Oh, do you! We won't say anything more about that, though I'm glad you'd like to have me along. Now then; go and have a good time! And take long steps and large mouthfuls! And you might do well to remember that a boy's stomach is not a birdnest to be lined with candy eggs."

"I think candy eggs would make a very good lining, better than real eggs; and about half the time you're trying to line me with them, aren't you? With all the sulphur in them! And I do hate sulphur, and I have always hated it since the boy at my desk in school wore a bag of it around his neck under his shirt to keep off diseases. My! how he smelt-worse than contagion! Candy eggs would make a very good lining; even the regular soldiers get candy in their rations now. And they don't have to eat new-laid eggs of mornings! Think of an army having to win a hard-fought battle on soft-boiled eggs! They don't have to do *that*, do they?"

"They do not!" said the doctor. "They positively do not! But we won't say anything more about eggs-saccharine or sulphurous. What are you going to do at the party?"

"I am going to dance."

"Alone? O dear! All alone? You'd better go skate on the ice! Not all alone?"

"I should say not! With my girl, of course."

"That's better, much better. And then what?"

"I am going to promenade, with my girl on my arm."

"On *both* arms, did you say?"

"No; on *one* arm."

"Which?"

"Either."

"That sounds natural! (Heart action regular; brain unclouded; temperature normal.) And then? What next?"

"I'm going to take the darling in to supper."

"Hold on! Not so fast! Suppose there isn't any supper-for the darling."

"Don't say that! It would nearly kill me! Don't you suppose there'll be any supper?"

"I'm afraid there will be. Well, after the darling has had her fatal supper? (Of course you won't want any!) What then?"

"What else is there to do?"

"You don't look as innocent as you imagine!"

"You don't have to confess what you'd like to do, do you? Would you have told your father?"

"I don't think I would."

"Then I won't tell you."

"Then you needn't! I don't wish to know-only it must *not* be on the cheek! Remember, you are no son of mine if it's on the cheek!"

"I thought I heard you say *that* got people into trouble."

"Maybe I did. I ought to have said it if I didn't; and it seems to be the kind of trouble that you are trying to get into. (Temperature rising but still normal. Respiration deeper. All symptoms favorable. No further bulletins deemed necessary.) Well, then? Where were we?"

"Anyhow, I've never thought of cheeks when I've thought of *that*; I thought cheeks were for chewing."

"Guardian Powers of our erring reason! Where did you get that idea-if sanity can call it an idea?"

"Watching our cows."

The doctor laughed till tears ran down his face.

"You can't learn much about kissing by watching anybody's *cows*, Governor," he said, wiping the tears away. "Not about *human* kissing. You must begin to direct your attention to an animal not so meek and drivable. You must learn to consider, my son, that hornless wonder and terror of the world who forever grazes but never ruminates!"

For years, in talking with a mind too young wholly to understand, he had enjoyed the play of his own mind. He knew only too well that there are few or none with whom a physician may dare have his sportive fling at his fellow-creatures, at life in general. From a listener who never sat in harsh judgment and who would never miscarry his random words, he had upon occasion derived incalculable relief.

"Anyhow, I have learned that cows have the new American way of chewing; so they never get indigestion, do they?"

"If they do, they cannot voice their symptoms in my mummied ears," said the doctor, who often seemed to himself to have been listening to hue and cry for medicine since the days of Thotmes. "However, we won't say anything further about *that*! What else are you going to do over there? This can't possibly be all!"

"To-night we children are going to sit up until midnight, to see whether the animals bellow and roar and make all kinds of noise on Christmas Eve. We know they don't, but we're going to *prove* they don't!"

"Where did you pick up that notion?"

"Where did you pick it up when you were a boy?"

"I fail to remember," admitted the doctor with mock dignity, damaged in his logic but recalling the child legend that on the Night of the Nativity universal nature was in sympathy with the miracle. All sentient creatures were wakeful and stirring, and sent forth the chorus of their cries in stables and barns-paying their tribute to the Divine in the Manger and proclaiming their brotherhood with Him who was to bring into the world a new gospel for them also.

"I don't know where I got that," he repeated. "Well, after the animals bellow and roar and make all kinds of noise, then what?"

"There isn't but one thing more; but that is best of all!"

"You don't say! Out with it!"

"That is our secret."

The new decision of tone demonstrated that another stage had been reached in their intercourse. The boy had withdrawn his confidence; he had entered the ranks of his own generation and had taken his confidence with him. Personally, also, he had shut the gate of his mind and the gate was guarded by a will; henceforth it was to be opened by permission of the guard. Something in their lives was abruptly ended; the father felt like ending the talk.

"Very well, then; we won't say anything more about the secret. And now you had better run along."

"But I don't want to run along just yet. It will be a long time before I see you again; have you thought of that?"

He reversed his position so as to face the fire; and he crossed his feet out beyond the promontory of the doctor's knees and folded his arms on the rampart of those enfolding arms.

For a few moments there was intimate silence. Then he inquired: —

"How old must a boy be to ask a girl?"

A flame more tender and humorous burned in the doctor's eyes.

"Ask her *what*?"

"Ask her nothing! Ask *her*!"

"You mean *tell* her, don't you? Not ask her, my friend and relative; *tell* her!"

"Well, ask her and tell her, too; they go together!"

"Is it possible! I'm always glad to learn!"

"Then, how old must he be?"

"Well, if you stand in need of the opinion of an experienced physician, as soon as he learns to speak would be about the right period! That would be the safest age! The patient would then have leisure to consider his case before being affected by the disease. You could have time to get singed and step away gradually instead of being roasted alive all at once. Does that sound hard?"

"Not very! Do you love a girl longer if you tell her or if you don't tell her?"

"I'm afraid nobody has ever tried *both* ways! Suppose you try both, and let us have the benefit of your experience."

"Well, then, if you love, do you love forever?"

The doctor laughed nervously and tightened his arms around the innocent.

"Nobody has lived forever yet-nobody knows!"

"But forever while you live-do you love as long as that?"

"You wouldn't know until you were dead and then it would be too late to report. But aren't you doing a good deal of hard fighting this morning, —on soft-boiled eggs, —though I think the victory is yours, General, the victory is truly and honestly yours!"

"I can't stop thinking, can I? You don't expect me to stop thinking, do you, when I'm just beginning really to think?"

"Very well, then, we won't say anything more about thinking."

"Then do you or don't you?"

"Now, what are you trying to talk about?" demanded the doctor angrily, and as if on instant guard. A new hatred seemed coming to life in him; there was a burning flash of it in his eyes.

"Just between ourselves-suppose that when I am a man and after I have been married to Elizabeth awhile, I get tired of her and want a little change. And I fell in love with another man's wife and dared not tell her, because if I did I might get a bullet through me; would I love the other man's wife more because I could not tell her, or would I love her more because I told her and risked the bullet?"

Pall-like silence draped the room, thick, awful silence. The father lifted his son from his lap to the floor, and turned him squarely around and looked him in the eyes imperiously. Many a time with some such screened but piercing power he, as a doctor, had scrutinized the faces of children to see whether they were aware that some vast tragedy of life was in the room with them. To keep them from knowing had often been his main care; seeing them know had been life's last pity; young children finding out the tragedies of their parents with one another-so many kinds of tragedies.

"You had better go now," he urged gently. Then an idea clamped his brain in its vise.

"And remember: while you are over there, you must try to behave with your best manners because you are going to stay in the house of a great lady. All the questions that you want to ask, ask me when you come back. Ask *me!*"

The boy standing before his father said with a strange quietness and stubbornness, probing him deeply through the eyes: —

"You haven't answered my *last* question yet, have you?"

"Not yet," said the doctor, with strange quietness also.

The boy had never before heard that tone from his father.

"It's sad being a doctor, isn't it?" he suggested, studying his father's expression.

"What do *you* know about sad? Who told *you* anything about sad?" muttered the doctor with new sadness now added to old sadness.

"Nobody *had* to tell me! I knew without being told."

"Run along now."

"Now I'll walk along, but I won't run along. I'll walk away from you, but I won't run away from you."

He wandered across the room, and stood with his hand reluctantly turning the knob. Then with a long, silent look at his father-he closed the door between them.

Dr. Birney stood motionless in the middle of the room with his gaze riveted on the door through which his son had lingeringly disappeared.

Some one of the world's greatest painters, chancing to enter, might worthily have desired to paint him-putting no questions as to who the man was or what he was; or what darkening or brightening history stretched behind him; or what entanglement of right and wrong lay around and within: painting only the unmistakable human signs he witnessed, and leaving his portrait for thousands of people to look at afterwards and make out of it what they could-through kinship with the good and evil in themselves: Velasquez, with his brush moving upon those areas of lonely struggle which sometimes lie with their wrecks at the bottom of the sea of human eyes; Franz Hals, fixing the cares which hover too long around our mouths; Vandyck, sitting in the shadow of the mystery that slants across all mortal shoulders; Rembrandt, drawn apart into the dignity that invests colossal disappointment. Any merciless, masterful limner of them all in a mood to portray those secret passions which drive men, especially men of middle age, towards safer deeps upon the rocks.

He had a well-set soldierly figure and the swarthy roughened face that results from years of exposure to weather —a face looking as if inwardly scarred by the tempests of his character but unwrinkled by the outer years. Both face and figure breathed the silent impassiveness of the regular who has been through campaigns enough already but is enlisted for life and for whatsoever duty may bring; he standing there in some wise palpably draped in the ideals of his profession as the soldier keeps his standard waving high somewhere near his tent, to remind him of the greatness that he guards and of the greatness that guards him.

Not a tall man as men grow on that Kentucky plateau; and looking less than his stature by reason of being so strongly built, square-standing, ponderous; his muscles here and there perceivable under his loosely fitting sack-suit of dark-gray tweeds; so that out of respect for strength which is both manhood and manliness, your eye travelled approvingly over his proportions: measuring the heavy legs down to the boots; the heavy arms out to the wrists; the heavy square thick muscular warm hands; and the heavy torso up to the short neck rising full out of a low turned-down collar.

In this neck an animal wildness and virile ferocity-not subdued, not stamped out, partly tamed by a will. Overtopping this neck a tremendous head covered with short glossy black hair, curling blue-black hair. In this head a powerful blunt nose, set like the muzzle of a big gun pointed to fire a heavy projectile at a distant target-the nose of a never-releasing tenacity. Above this nose, right and left, thick black brows, the bars of nature's iron purpose. Under these brows wonderful grayish eyes with glints of Scotch blue in them or of Irish blue or of Saxon blue; for the blood of three races ran thick in his veins and mingled in the confusions of his character: blue that was in the eyes of earlier Scottish men, exulting in heather and highland stag; or the blue of other eyes that had looked meltingly on golden-haired minstrel and gold-framed harp-eyes that might have poured their love into Isolde's or have faded out in the death of Tristan; or the blue of still other eyes-archers who had shot their last arrows and, dying, drew themselves to the feet of Harold, their blue-eyed king fighting for Saxon England's right and might.

They were eyes that could look you to the core with intelligence and then rest upon you from the outside with sympathy for all that he had seen to be human in you whether of strength or of weakness-but never of meanness. Under the blunt nose a thick stubby mustache trimmed short, leaving exposed the whole red mouth-the mouth of great passions-no paltry passions-none despicable or contemptible.

On the whole a man who advances upon you with all there is in him and without waiting for you to advance upon him; no stepping aside for people in this world by this man, nor stepping timidly over things. Even as he stood there a motionless figure, he diffused an influence most warm and human, gay and tragic, irresistible. A man loved secretly or openly by many women.

A man that men were glad to come to confide in, when they crossed the frontiers of what Balzac, speaking of the soldiers of Napoleon, called their miserable joys and joyous miseries.

But assuredly not a man to be put together by piecemeal description such as this: the very secret of his immense influence being some charm of mystery, as there is mystery in all the people that win us and rule us and hold us; as though we pressed our ear against this mystery and caught there the sound of a meaning vaster than ourselves-not meant for us but flowing away from us along the unbroken channels of the universe: still to be flowing there long after we ourselves are stilled.

Thus he stood in his library that morning when his son left him, brought to a stop in the road of life as by a straw fallen at his feet borne on a rising wind-another harbinger of a coming storm.

By and by not far away a door on that side of the house was slammed. The sound of muffled feet was heard on the porch and then the laughter of children as they bounded across the yard. As his ear caught the noises, he hurried to the window and looked out; and then he threw up the sash and hailed them loudly: —

"Ho, there! you winter snow-birds without wings!"

As the children wheeled and paused, he smiled and shook his forefinger: —

"Remember to keep those two red mouths closed and to breathe through those two red noses!" and then as he recalled some exercises which he had lately been putting them through, he added with ironic emphasis, laughing the while: —

"And when you breathe, remember to bring into play those two invaluable little American diaphragms and those two priceless pairs of American ribs!"

The little girl nodded repeatedly to indicate that she could understand if she would and would obey if she cared; and putting her red-mittened finger-tips to her lips, she threw him a good-by with a wide sweeping gesture of the arms to right and left. And the boy made a soldierly salute, touching a hand to his skull-cap with the uncouth rigor of a veteran in the raw: then they bounded off again.

The doctor drew down the sash and watched them.

A hundred yards from the house the ground sloped to a limestone spring at the foot of the hill —a characteristic Kentucky formation. From this spring issued a brook, on the banks of which stood a clump of forest trees, bathing their roots in the moisture. Upon reaching the brow of this hill, the boy lagged behind his sister as though to elude her observation; then turning looked back at his father-looked but made no sign: a little upright pillar of life on the brow of that declivity: then he dropped out of sight.

A few moments later up over the hill where he was last seen a little cloud of autumn leaves came scurrying. As they neared the wall of the house where the wind by pressure veered skyward to clear the roof, some of the leaves were caught up and dashed against the windowpanes behind which the doctor was standing. Had the sash been raised, they would have thrown themselves into his arms and have clung to his neck and breast.

He did not know why, but they caused him a pang: those little brown parchments torn from the finished volume of the year: they caused him a subtle pang.

He turned from the window, goaded by more than resolution, and crossed to his writing-desk on the opposite side: there lay the work mapped out for the morning. No interruptions were to be expected from his patients, though of course there might be new patients since accidents and illnesses befall unheralded. There would be no visitors-not to-day. In a country of the warmest social customs and of family ties so widely interknit that whole communities are bound together as with vine-like closeness, no one visits on the day before Christmas. In every little town the world of people crowd the streets and shops or busy themselves in preparations at home: out in the country those who have not flocked to the towns are as joyously occupied. No visitors, then. And the children were gone-no disturbances from their romping. The servants had put his rooms in order, and were too discreetly trained to return upon their paths.

After breakfast, at the stable, he had given orders to his man for the day while he was having a look at his horses-well-stalled, well-groomed, docile, intelligent: at his gaited saddle-horse, at the nag for his buggy, at the perfectly matched pair for his carriage. As he appeared in the doorway of the stalls, each beast, turning his head, had sent to him its affectionate greeting out of eyes that looked like wells of soft blue smoke: each said, "Take me to-day."

He was a little vain of being weatherwise, as is apt to be the case with country-bred folk: and at the last stable door, having studied the wind and the sky and the temperature, he had said to his man that the weather was changing: it would be snowing by afternoon. Usually in that latitude the first flurry of snow gladdens the eye near Thanksgiving, but sleighs are not often flying until late in December. There had been no snow as yet; it was due, and the weather showed signs of its multitudinous onset.

He felt so sure in his forecast that he had instructed his man to put the sleigh in readiness. He himself went into the saddle-house and from a peg amid the gear and harness he took down the sleighbells. As he shook them roughly, he smiled as above that cascade of mellow winter sounds there settled a little cloud of summer dust. He observed that the leather needed mending-what he called "a few surgical stitches"; and he had brought the bells with him to the house and they now lay on the floor of his office in the adjoining room.

He thought that if it should snow heavily enough he would use the sleigh when he started out in the afternoon. There were several sick children to visit on opposite horizons of his neighborhood. The sound of the bells as he drove in at their front gates might have value: it would not only mean the coming of his sleigh, but it would suggest to them the approach of that mysterious Sleigh of the World which that night they were expecting. Afterwards he was to go to a distant county seat for a consultation. His road home was a straight turnpike: it would be late when he returned, perhaps far in the night; and he would have the sound of the bells to himself-the bells and his thoughts and Christmas Eve.

This plan of Dr. Birney's regarding the children laid bare one of his ideas as a physician. For years he had employed increasingly in his practice the power of suggestion. For years life as he sometimes surmised had employed the power of suggestion on him. He felt assured that in treating the sick there are cases where every suggestion of happiness that can reach a patient draws him back toward life: every suggestion of unhappiness lowers his vitality and helps to roll him over the precipice: the final push need be a very slight one. The melody of sleighbells falling on the ears of the sick children that afternoon might have the weight of a sunbeam on delicate scales and tip the balances as he wished: he believed that many a time the weight of a mental sunbeam was all that was needed to decide the issue.

He looked at his watch. It was ten o'clock, and dinner was served at one, and he had a tranquil outlook for three hours of work. The only remaining source from which an interruption could have reached him was his wife. His wife! —his wife never-intruded.

Not three hours, but two hours and a half, to be exact; for the dining-room adjoined his library, and every day at half past twelve o'clock his wife entered the dining-room to superintend final preparations for dinner: from the instant of her entrance concentration of mind ended for him: he occupied himself with things less important and with odds and ends for mind and body.

She would draw the shades of the windows delicately to temper the light according as the day was cloudy or cloudless; she would bring fresh flowers for the table; she would inspect the clearness of the cut glass, the brightness of the silver, the snowiness of the napkins; she would prepare at the sideboard a salad, a sauce; she would give a final push to the chairs-last of all a straightening push to his. All the lower drudgery of the servants and all the higher domestic triumphs of her skill led to his chair-as to a kind of throne where the function of feeding reigned. With that final adjustment of the piece of furniture in which his body was to be at ease while it gorged itself, with that act of grade, the doors were opened; dinner was announced; he walked in, and faced his wife, and dined-with Nemesis.

This pride of hers in housekeeping was part of her inheritance, of the civilization of her land and people: it was a little separate dynasty of itself. Often as the years had gone by he had been thankful that she could thus far find compensation for larger disappointment; it helped to keep her a healthy woman if it could not render her a happy wife. Near the sugar and the flour she could perhaps three times a day realize small perfections; she could mould little ideals and turn them out on the shelf and verify them with a silver spoon: an ideal life in the pantry for a woman who had expected an ideal life with him in library and parlor and bedroom and out in the world. It was all as if she sat at the base of Love's ruined Pyramids and tried to divert her desolation by configuring ant hills.

And he was well aware that this pride of housekeeping was the least of all the prides that grouped themselves around that central humiliation of wifehood. He had sometimes thought that if, after her death, over her were planted a weeping willow, mere nutritive pride in her dust would force the boughs to reverse their natural direction and shoot upward as stiff as a spruce.

The dining-room, in the old-fashioned Kentucky way, was richly carpeted; but the moment she set her foot within it, he could trace her steps as unerringly as though she had been shod with explosives. Likewise she sang to herself a good deal: (he had long ago diagnosed that symptom of nervous self-consciousness).

When he had married her, voice and piano had been one of the resources he thought he would hold in reserve for the emptying years; music would fill so much rational silence. It was one of his semi-serious declarations that only two people more or less out of their senses could keep on talking to each other till death forced them to hold their tongues. But with tragic swiftness and sureness a few years after their marriage the music stopped, the piano was shut.

More than that terminated. After two children were born, there were no more: that profound living music came to an end also. And perhaps one of the deepest desires of his nature was for that kind of long union with his wife and for many children: perhaps the only austerity in him was an austere patriarchal authority to people the earth and to bequeath the inheritance of it to his seed.

When she had ceased singing to him soon after marriage, she had begun to sing to herself- habitually during this half-hour of proximity. The sound took up a fixed abode in his ear as there is a roaring in a seashell. He could hear it miles across the country; it was the loudest sound to him in this world-that barely audible self-conscious singing of his wife.

During this interval also she addressed her commands to the maid in tones lowered not to disturb him. He could not hear the words, but there was no mistaking the tones! What beautiful, eager, victorious, thrilling tones-over a dish of steaming vegetables-over a savory toast! They forced him to be reminded that the nature of his wife was not a brook run dry; its leaping waters were merely turned away into another channel. Only when she spoke with him did the cadence of her tones sag; then all the modulations ran downhill as into some inner pit of emptiness.

It was impossible for him to believe that the occasional chuckle and cackle of the maid during these whispered colloquies grew out of aspersions winged at him-at the hungry ogre, middle-aged, almost corpulent, on the other side of the wall; at the species of advanced gorilla, poorly disguised in collar and necktie and midway garments; and with wool and leather drawn over his lower pair of modernized walking hands! Yet the truth was undeniable that when dinner was announced and he went in, the maid, standing behind her mistress's chair, fixed her gaze on him with fresh daily delight in understanding or misunderstanding the wretchedness of the household.

The first time he had ever seen this maid was one evening upon going in to supper. They were expecting guests, and his wife wore an evening gown. As he seated himself, he became aware almost without glancing across the table that something novel had arrived upon the scene- something youthful yet as immemorial as Erebus. Behind the glistening whiteness of his wife's bust with its cold proud dignity, there was something sable-birdlike-all beak and eyes-with a small head on which grew a kind of ruffled indignant feathers. He tried to take no further notice of the apparition, but could not escape the experience that several times during the meal he rescued his biscuit as from between the claws of a competing raven.

In the course of time, as this combination of black and white refused to dissolve and rather coalesced into a duality holding good for meal hours, he felt impelled to characterize the alliance- to envisage for his own relief the totality of its comic gloom. So he called it his *Bust of Pallas* and his *Nevermore*. And his *Nevermore*, perched behind his *Bust of Pallas* at every function, fixed her dull stupid eyes on him in unceasing judgment. He was never quite persuaded of the human reality of her; never fully believed that she reached to the carpet: and he never got up from the table to see whether she cast a shadow on the floor; but he knew that it was the fowl's intention to cast whatsoever shadow it carried about with it *upon him*.

She had become a critic of his domestic relations. This servant, this mal-arrangement of beak and eyes, with bare brain enough not to let plates fall and not to dangle her fingers in scalding water nor singe her head-feathers in the oven-this servant of his arraigned *him* in his humanity! And if this servant, then all his servants. And if all his servants, then all the servants of the neighborhood. The whole Plutonian shore croaked its black damnation of him. Of *him*! —the leading citizen of his community, its central vital character who held in his keeping the destiny of a people! He had a vision of the august assemblage of them uplifted into the heavenliness of an African Walhalla-such as is disclosed in the last act of the *Tetralogy* —all gazing down upon him as a profaning Alberic who had raped the virgin Gold of marital love.

On a near peak of especial moral grandeur, his *Nevermore* stood in her supernal resentment of his wife's wrong. For whatever *Nevermore* was not, at least, she was woman. And what woman fails to espouse any wife's dignity except the woman who supplants the wife? (Not even she; for if ever in turn her hour comes, her first outcry is, 'I might have known.')

Dr. Birney did not have three hours for this morning's business, then, but two hours and a half; and forthwith beginning, he took from his breast-pocket a small book and transferred from it to a large diary his notes of visits to patients on the day preceding. This soon done, he was ready for the main work.

It was now the closing week of the year when according to custom he posted the year's books; for he was his own secretary. By New Year's Day his accounts were about ready and new books were opened.

He always took up with repugnance this valuation of his services. It was to him one of life's ironies that in order to live he must take toll of death. He must harvest his bread from the fields of tears. He must catch his annual treasure from those rainbows of hope that spanned weary pillows. He must fill his wine-jar by dipping his cup into the waves of Lethe. He must equip his very stable with the ferriage he had collected on the banks of the Styx.

His heart was never in his bookkeeping; this morning he could barely fix upon it his thoughts; so that before commencing he allowed himself to turn the leaves, getting a distasteful bird's-eye view of this panorama of neighborhood suffering and mortality there outspread on the table.

Two infants in January had had scarlet fever; so much for the infants and the fever. A boy had had measles; an assessment for measles. A girl had had mumps; the price of mumps. An old lady, going one bitter February afternoon to her hen-house to see whether the hens had begun to lay, had slipped on the ice-covered step and had fractured her hip-bone; damages for the friable hip-bone of the senile. A negro man, stationed in an ice-house to knock to pieces with an axe the blocks of ice as they were hauled from the pond, had had his feet frost-bitten. In April a stable-boy had been kicked in the groin and bitten in the shoulder by a stallion. This stallion, in whom survived the fighting traits of the wild horse and defiance of man as an enemy who had no use for him but to enslave him and work him to death, had already killed two stablemen. Too valuable for the stud to be himself killed, and too dangerous to be approached or handled, it was decided to destroy his eyesight; and the doctor had been called in to treat both stable-boy and stallion. There was a bill for his services to the boy; none for the stallion; he was not a veterinary. But it was his hand that had jabbed the long needle into those virile unconquerable eyes-leaving that Samson Agonistes of the herd whose only crime had been to reject civilization, as was his right. There was no one to put out the doctor's eyes, who also had rejected civilization: which was not his right.

In June a lad, climbing a cherry tree with the ambition to capture the earliest cherries dangling scarlet, had fallen flat upon his back when the limb had split from the half-rotten trunk, thus jarring his spine. It was a bad case; he must now make out a good bill for it, otherwise the father would feel resentful.

In harvest time one of his friends, a young farmer, overheated, went bathing too soon in a fresh-water pond-made cooler by a recent hail-storm; between the leaves lay a note from his widow, with its deep black border and its mourning perfume; she had asked for the account-had asked punctiliously to pay for a beloved young husband's fatal chill. In autumn two barefoot half-grown brothers were cutting ironweeds in a pasture with hemphooks; the elder by too heavy a stroke had sent his blade clean through a clump of weeds into the ankle of the younger, slashing it to the bone.

Thus the record ran on as the doctor turned the pages in a preliminary survey of his chart of suffering. And then there were the cases of those coming into the world and the cases of those going out: birth-rates, death-rates. He must exact of Nature his fee for continuing the existence of the human race; and he must go about among his friends and neighbors and wring money out of them because those they loved best had merely paid their own decent debt to mortality.

He dipped his pen into the ink, drew before him some blanks, and began to make out the bills. The rooms were very quiet and comfortable; winter sunshine entered through the windows; the Christmas wind frolicked outside the walls.

To be forced to sit there and say to the world: My feelings have nothing to do with it: you must pay what you owe! Because all life is payment; everything is a settlement. There is but one that is exempt-Nature. It is only she who never fails to collect a debt but who never pays one. Who that has ever lived our common human life, borne its burdens, felt its cares, fought against its wrongs, who but knows that Nature is in debt to him? But what son of hers has ever been able to tear his due from her!

More may be learned about the doctor by an inspection of his rooms. Of these there were three, with a small fourth chamber as an ell in the house: in this ell there was a single bed, and here he sometimes slept-as nearly outside the house as it was possible to lie and still to be within it.

The room in which he now worked was his library; communicating through an open door was his office; beyond the office through another open door was a third room in which were stored many personal articles of indoor and outdoor use.

Beginning with his office, you derived the knowledge which any physician's and surgeon's office, if modern and complete, should afford. On one wall hung his diploma from a New York Medical College; on another a diploma from Vienna for post-graduate study and hospital work.

The rooms taken together bore testimony in their entire equipment to a general outside truth: that the physician who lived in them was not a country doctor because he had been crowded by abler members of the profession out of the cities where there are many into the country where there are none: and this fact in turn had its larger historic significance.

Almost within a generation a radical change has taken place in the relation of town and country as regards the profession of medicine. The old barriers which half a century ago separated the sick in the streets from the sick in fields and forests have been swept away. The city physician now twenty-five miles away can often arrive more quickly than a country doctor who lives five; and a surgeon can come in an hour who formerly needed half a day. But many now living with long memories can well remember the time when the country doctor ruled in his neighborhood as the priest in mediæval Europe swayed his parish. However remote, he was always sent for. His form was the very image of rescue, his face was the light of healing. As a consequence, the country often developed leaders in the profession. Instead of its being dependent upon the cities, these looked to the rural districts for many of the most skilful practitioners.

This was strikingly true from the earliest settlement of the West on that immense plateau of forest and grass land which has long since drawn to itself the notice of the world as the loveliness of Kentucky. It was on the southern boundary of this plateau, living in a pioneer hamlet and practising far and wide through a wilderness, that a country doctor became the father of ovarian surgery in the United States and won the reverence of the world of science and the gratitude of humanity. In another pioneer settlement one of the greatest of American lithotomists spread the lustre of his name and the goodness of his deeds over the whole country west of the Alleghany Mountains; and these were but two of those many country doctors who there for well-nigh a century were the reliance of their people: physicians, surgeons, diagnosticians, nurses, pharmacists, friends-all in one.

This powerful and brilliant tradition had descended to Dr. Birney, and he had worthily upheld it. In some respects he had solidly advanced it, notably in his treatment of children's diseases.

A second room, in which the articles of his personal life were kept, gave further knowledge of him as a man. Outside the windows there was a tennis court; he played tennis with his children and with young people of the neighborhood. You saw his racquet on the wall; and if you had opened a closet, you would have found the flannels and the shoes. Elsewhere on the wall you saw his reel. In season he liked to fish, when his patients also could go fishing, or at least were well enough to feel like going; and in the same closet you might have noted the residue of a fisherman's outfit. He fished not only for black bass, but for that mild pond and creek fish prized as a delicacy on Kentucky tables —a variety of the calico bass known in the local vocabulary as "newlight."

Still elsewhere you saw his game bag and bird gun-he liked to call it by the older word, fowling-piece. He hunted: quail, doves, wild duck. In another closet you would have been interested to discover his regalia as a member of the Order of Masons; and well placed beside it his uniform as a member of the State Guard-the two well placed there. When years before his neighbors had enrolled him in the Guard, they had saluted him as one more Kentucky Colonel. "I will submit to no official degradation," he had said; "I am already the Commander of the whole army of you on the field of your human Waterloo: salute your General!"

His library added its testimony as to other humanities. Scattered about on tables and mantelpiece were fine old pipes and boxes of cigars and playing-cards. There were poker chips, showing that the doctor had poker neighbors (where else if not there?), though whist was his game. You realized that he was a man at home among a people who loved play-must have play. On his sideboard were temperate decanters: he had sideboard neighbors. Altogether a human-looking room for much that is human; easy to enter, comfortable to stay in, hard to quit.

But our closest friends can come so close to us and no closer; they surround us but none of them enters us. Nature forbids that any but our own feet should cross the bridge spanning the distance between other people and the fortress of the individual. Across that bridge we can take with us no companions except those that keep silent amid its silences; that can speak to us but that cannot see us: those great voices without eyes; those great listeners without ears; great counsellors without criticism; great hands that guide and refuse to smite; great judges that embody law and refuse to sit in judgment on us-Books.

Some of the doctor's books held for him life's indispensable laughter; and no one of us ever tells all the things in this world that we laugh at. Some held for him life's tears; and no one of us ever tells the things that secretly start our own. Some held neither laughter nor tears but what is above both-life's calm; and what one of us but at times feels the need to ascend to some inner mountain-top of our own spirits-far above the whole darkened or radiant cloud-rack of emotion-and look futureward into the promised peace, the end of our wandering. Joys-sorrows-and calm: these three for him, too.

Such books stayed with the doctor year after year. He could wake in the night and find them through the darkness; in the darkness they knew how to find him. They were not part of his medical library, of course, which was another matter. But they filled three sides of a large low revolving bookcase in the middle of the room beside his easy chair and his lamp and table.

The fourth side of his bookcase held the books that came and went as a stream, entering and passing on: he drank from them as they flowed by. Always they were books of fiction or biography which held in solution the truth of the human matter about some life that had fought or was fighting its path through to victory. Always he would have books of victory. By preference it must be a story real or imagined of some boy, youth, young man, middle-aged man, who was in the struggle for existence and who was on the side of survival. He kept in mind the words of a great Frenchman that the way to make an impression upon the world is to plough through humanity like a cannon-ball or to creep through it like a pestilence. But he knew that in this world there are very few human cannonballs, though of such pestilence there is always more than enough. Rather every common man's life, and every uncommon man's life, is a drawn sword that has to cut its way through all other drawn swords. Here were the books which disclosed the mettle of a character: the last magnificent refusal to be ruined by evil which is the very breath of a man and the slow measure of the world's advance. So that, while much is always failing in everybody, all is never failing. Out of the blackest abyss there arises in the wounded and prostrate some white peak of unmelting innocence-at the base of which Life's battle rages.

Many a time long after midnight he would read to a finish some such triumphant story; and with a murmur of "Well done!" he would close the book, turn out his lamp, and go to sleep in his chair with his clothes on-with that scene of victory emptying its echoes into his ear and his dreams.

Here, then, was some discrete knowledge of the doctor as a doctor and as a man. But there was one thing in his library that blended these two separate aspects, showing how the man felt as a physician and how the physician felt as a man. This was a series of pictures running around the walls and connecting great epochs in the progress of Medicine.

He had a liking, as the world has, for some brief series of climaxes that will depict a subject at a glance. Very memorable to him was Shakespeare's Seven Ages-because they were seven and were thus easily grasped by poetry and reason. But he knew that Shakespeare might as truly have substituted another seven-with as good poetry and reason; or he might have made the ages fourteen or forty-nine or forty-nine hundred; for actually the ages of a man's life are infinite; but being reduced to seven, we all recognize them.

And memorable to him likewise had been Hogarth's *Progress of the Rake* with its few pictures; and his *Progress of the Harlot* with its few; and his *Progress of Marriage à la Mode* with its few; and the *Progress of Cruelty* with its fewest of all-only four, but more than enough! And yet the stages in the progress of the rake and of the harlot and of marriage à la mode and of cruelty are infinite; and at no single stage in the progress of any one of them could you actually find either Rake or Harlot or Infidelity or Cruelty. Being portrayed as few, the world understands and finds its own account in them.

So around the walls of his library there hung a series of pictures showing the progress of Medicine across the ages.

The first picture represented a scene in the life of primitive man, during the period when he had long enough been man to form into hostile tribes, but not long enough to have advanced far from the boundaries of the brute. It is a battle picture: the battle is over: the survivors are gone: the dead and wounded lie about. Medicine as a human science has not yet been born; surgery has not yet separated itself from the movements of instinct. Yet there was activity among the wounded. In some of the warriors you saw such attempts in the care of their wounds as one may witness to-day in wounded birds and animals-if one is fortunate enough to be so placed as to be able to watch: there were the instinctive devices to cleanse, to protect, to alleviate: those low beginnings of the great science which you may observe to-day in your dog when he has come home after a fight with lacerated ears and slashed thighs-when he crawls under the porch to the darkest corner to keep away other dogs and light and flies; whose sole instrument of cleansing is his tongue and whose only bathing fluid is saliva. On that battle-field you saw such beginnings of surgery as to-day is practised by a bird treating its broken wing or broken leg. Thus the wounded warriors concerned themselves with their hurts-all mother-naked. Along one edge of the battle-field was a stream of running water; some had started to draw themselves toward this and had died on the way. One was stretched full alongside —a young chief of magnificent proportions and a face of higher intelligence. And out of that intelligence, as a marvellous advance in the development of man, you saw one action: he was dipping up water in the palm of his hand and pouring it upon his wound. At some moment in the history of the race there must somewhere have been that first movement of the developing animal to substitute water for saliva. That great historic moment was depicted there. It was still the Azoic Age of Medicine.

Near by hung a second picture. Ages have passed, no one knows how many. The brute has become Prometheus; he has learned the use of fire; and he has learned the most heroic application of flame-to touch it to himself where he is in greatest agony: that is, he has learned to cauterize his wounds. More than fire can he now handle; he has learned to bring together fat and flame; and he has discovered how from flame to produce oil; and he has learned to pour boiling oil into the holes in his body made by the implements of war. It is the long Ages of Medicine for the cautery and burning oil.

A third picture hung next. More ages have passed, no one knows how many; and the scene is another battle-field far down toward modern times. It is France; it is the second half of the sixteenth century; it is warfare in Piedmont. Troops are sweeping up the hill, and in the background is a walled city with turrets and towers; and in the foreground wounded soldiers are arriving or are lying about on the ground. There is a rude mass of masonry used as an operating-table; and on the operating-table is a soldier, one of whose legs has just been amputated above the knee; an attendant holds the saw with which the leg has just been sawed off, and the stump of it has dropped below. Beside the wounded man stand two figures: one the figure of the past; and the other a figure of the future —a poor barber's apprentice, father of modern surgery, named to be massacred on St. Bartholomew's eve, but spared because none but a despised Huguenot could be found in all France skilful enough to safeguard the royal orthodox blood. There beside the soldier they stand, these two, and in them ages meet; for the figure of the past holds in his hand one of the cauteries that are kept redhot in a brazier near his feet; and the other holds in his a new thing in the world —a simple ligature. A great scene, a great epoch: the beginning of new surgery when the flowing of blood from amputations of the great arteries could be stopped by a mere bandage: that man-Ambroise Paré!

More centuries have passed-we know exactly how many now from year to year. It is the nineteenth, and it is the New World; the next picture on the library wall portrayed a scene on the Western frontier of a new civilization. It is the backwoods of Kentucky, it is a pioneer settlement of three or four hundred souls, nearly a thousand miles from any hospital or dissecting-room. In the front door of his rude pioneer house stands a Kentucky country doctor, Ephraim MacDowell. His patient is before him, a woman on horseback in a side-saddle. She has just arrived, having ridden some seventy miles through the wilderness. He is assisting her to alight; and he is soon to perform, without consultation, without precedent in the ages of surgery (but not without a prayer for himself and her), by strength of his own will and nerve and by the light of the solitary candle of his own genius, an operation which made Kentucky the mother of ovarian surgery for all coming time, a new epoch of life and mercy: he going his own way to immortality as Shakespeare went his, as the greatest always go theirs-by a new path untrumpeted and alone.

Another picture represented a scene in Boston in 1846, less than half a century later; for the lonely mountain peaks of progress stretching across the ages are beginning to crowd each other now; they are beginning to run together into a range of continuous discovery. That picture also shows an operating-room; and there stood the American Morton, making for the world the first merciful use of anæsthetics: with which the silence of painlessness fell upon humanity's old outcry of torture under treatment.

There the doctor's pictures ended. In our own time he might have added one more for the epoch of the Roentgen Ray and another for the Finsen Light; and another for transfusion of blood; and still others crowning other mountain-tops in the new Surgery and new Medicine.

Thus he had before his eyes in his library some few Ages of his Science-as it went forward and slipped back and missed the road and forgot the road, yet somehow steadily advanced across the centuries like an erring unconquerable man across his years. Not progressing however as a man grows, from infancy to decrepitude; but moving from its old age toward its youth, always toward its youth, as Swedenborg's Angels fly forever toward their Spring. It ran around his walls like a great roadway, connecting the last discoveries of his Science with the surgery of the wolf who gnaws off his imprisoned leg and with the medicine of the sick dog that eats grass.

He called it his World's Path of Lessening Pain.

It was the last refuge and solace of his often tired and often wounded mind. Even after friends were gone at night and the poker chips were stacked or the whist counters folded; after the sideboard had been visited and temperately forsaken; after the abiding books had done for him what they could; in the still house far into the night, he would sometimes lie back in his chair and survey those battle-pictures of a science on which he was spending his loyalty and his strength.

Once, in younger days, outside the Eternal City, he had gone to study those fragments of the Old Roman Aqueduct that to-day are slowly crumbling on the Campagna; and standing alone before it he had in imagination searched for the figure of some young workman who had helped to mould those brick or to finish those columns: the figure of some obscure vanished peasant. So the great wall of his science, being built onward across the centuries into the future, would be revisited by men of the future in places where it stood in ruins. He would be as one whose life with its mistakes was yet linked to indestructible good. He would vanish from beside the wall himself, but his work upon it would have helped to uphold humanity. And many a night he went asleep in his chair, committing himself to his Science, as the forgotten Roman laborer of old may have fallen asleep under his own arch.

But, in that same Italy, northward are the Apennines; and sometimes in travelling through these or through the Swiss glaciers where Nature measures all things on the scale of the sublime-sometimes as your eye is passing from snow peak to snow peak, suddenly away up on some mountain-side you will see a human hut; and standing in the door of that hut a single human being; and the thought may come to you that there, in the heart of that pygmy, may dwell sorrow that dwarfs the Alps.

The doctor's library had such a picture: it completed the story of the room, and it effaced everything else in it. In a somewhat darkened corner hung a framed photograph of his wife in her bridal dress made not long after their wedding. Once his photograph had hung beside it. The plaster where the nail had been driven in had either fallen out or it had been torn out. He never knew-he knew enough not to ask.

As for the photograph, there stood a young bride, looking into her future and trying to conceal from herself what she saw soon awaiting her: the life of a woman wedded but not loved. And there was recollection in the eyes too: that the man who had married her perhaps in the very breath of his wooing had wished she were another; that at the altar he had perhaps wished he were putting his ring upon another's hand; and that if there were to be children, he would always be wishing for them another mother.

The doctor sat there that morning trying to work at the books of the year. The rooms were comfortable; the children were away at the fireside of another man's wife; the servants did not dare disturb him; his horses waited in their stalls; it was the day on which he could begin to reap his golden harvest —a pleasant day for most men; but he could not see the blanks before him nor remember the names he filled in nor the figures that were for value received.

Because there lay open before him the Book of the Years.

And coming down toward him on the track of memory through this book was his life from boyhood to middle age: first the playing feet of the child that have no path as yet; then the straight path of the boy; then the winding road of youth; then the quickly widened road, so smooth, so easy, of a young man; and then the fixed deepening rut of middle age.

And now the rut of middle age had come to its forks: north fork and south fork; or east fork and west fork-he must choose.

Whoso cares to know where and how the doctor's life-path started and across what kind of country it had run until now, a middle-aged man, he sat there this day at the tragedy of its forking, may if he so choose follow the road by the chart of a narrative.

But let him remember that this narrative goes back into a society unlike that of to-day and into a Kentucky that has vanished. Back there are other manners, other customs, other types of men: a different light on the world altogether.

IV. The Book of the Years

More than half a century ago, or during the decade of 1850 and 1860, when American life on the fertile plain of Kentucky attained its ripest flavor, there was living with great ease to himself and others on a large estate in one of the bluegrass counties a country gentleman and farmer who was nothing more: nothing more because that was enough. Being farmer took up much of his time, and being a gentleman took up the rest.

He one day observed that his prolific heels were beginning to be trodden upon by a group of stalwart sons nearing manhood; or, in the idiom of that picturesque soil, all thickly bunched in their race for the grand stand. According to the robust family life of that era and people, a year or less was often the interval between births; and a father, slanting his eyes upward to his oldest who had just reached twenty-one, might catch a glimpse of a fourth son smiling loyally at him from the top of the rank stalk of eighteen.

This juvenescent and prodigal sire clearly foreseeing, as many of his neighbors foresaw, the emancipation of the negroes and the downfall of the Southern feudal system and thus the downfall of the Kentucky gentleman of the feudal soil, could see no further. When those grapes then ripening went into the winepress of destiny, there would be no more like them: the stock would be cut down, a new vineyard would have to be planted; and what might become of his sons as laborers in that vineyard he knew not, though looking wistfully forth. Therefore he determined to store them away for their own safeguard among those ancestral professions alike of the Old and New World that are exempt from political vicissitude and dynastic changes.

Now it happened that among his friends he counted the great Dr. Benjamin Dudley, the illustrious Kentucky lithotomist at Lexington; and taking counsel of that learned and kindly man, he chose for his first-born stalwart-since the stalwart when invited to do so declined to choose it for himself-the profession of medicine; and having politely packed his trunk, he politely packed him with a polite body servant and a polite good-by off to a medical school, the best the Southern States then boasted-and the Southern States knew how to boast in those days.

But the colt that has been dragged to the water cannot be forced to drink; and the semi-docile son could not be made to introduce into his system his father's professional prescription. His presence at the medical school was evidence in its way that he had swallowed the prescription; but his conduct as a student showed that by his own will he had inhibited its action upon his vital parts.

In the year of finishing his course of lectures his father died; and upon returning home certificated as a doctor, he returned also as a young blood of independent fortune, independent future, and independent Feelings-the last of which, the Feelings, he regarded as by far the most important of the three. At the bottom of his trunk against the lining was his diploma, on the principle that we pack first what we shall need last.

The immediate use this golden youth made of his liberty and his Feelings was to take over into his control a share of the ancestral estate that fell to him under our American laws of partible inheritance; to build on it a low rambling manor house; and into this to convey his portion of the polished family silver and the polished family blacks. Soon afterward with no exertion on his part he married him a wife in the neighborhood; tore up his diploma as if to annihilate in his establishment the very recognition of disease; laid off a training-track; and proceeded to employ his languid energies in a fashion which his father had not favored for any of his sons-the breeding of Kentucky thoroughbreds.

Years passed. History came and went its thundering way, leaving the nation like a forest blasted with lightning and drenched with rain. The Kentucky gentleman of the feudal sort was gone, having disappeared in the clouds of that history which had swept him from the landscape.

The mild young Kentucky breeder mellowed to his middle years, winning and losing on the road as we all must, but with never a word about it one way or the other from him; early losing his wife and winning the makeshifts of widowerhood, entering so to speak upon its restrictions; losing his little daughter and winning a nephew whom he adopted and idolized; letting him run wild over the house, and then about the yard, and then about the farm, and then across boundary fences into other farms, and then into the towns, and then out into the world.

There were parts of his farm that looked like English downs; and on these fed Southdown sheep; for the Kentucky country gentleman of that period killed his own mutton. (He killed pretty much his own everything, even his own neighbors.) No saddle of mutton out of a public market house for him and for his groaning mahogany. And so it seemed well-nigh a romantic coincidence that the fatherless, motherless boy who came to play on these downs should have arrived there with the name of Downs Birney.

The Kentucky turfman, with his Southdown sheep and Durham cattle and White Berkshire hogs and thoroughbred horses and Blue-dorking chickens, was born, as may already have been observed, with that Southern indolence which occasionally equals the Oriental's; and as more time passed he settled into the deeper imperturbability of men who commit their destiny to fast horses. Apparently they early become so inoculated with hazard as to end in being immune to all excitement. As he could stroll over his farm without having to climb a hill, he had perhaps preferred to build him a low manor house so that he could lounge over it without having to take the trouble to go upstairs. In the chosen business of his life it would appear that he had wished to avail himself of a principle of Old Roman law: that he who does a thing through another does it himself; and thus he could sit perfectly still on his veranda with two legs and run nearly a mile a minute on a track with four.

A rural Kentucky gentleman of dead-ripe local pre-bellum flavor: exhaling a kind of Falernian bouquet as he dwelt under the serene blue sky on a beautiful bluegrass Sabine farm: a warm-visaged, soft-handed, bland-voiced man-so bland that when he strolled up to you and accosted you, you were uncertain whether he was going to offer to bet with you or to baptize you. Season after season this tranquil happy Kentuckian dwelt there, intent upon making nothing of himself and upon making the horse an adequate citizen of a state that likes to go its own gait-and to make him a leading citizen of the world: measurably he succeeded in doing both.

As he receded from view, his horses advanced into notice. He was probably never better satisfied with his stable lot and with his human lot than when at one of his annual sales he could hear the auctioneer-that high-gingered Pindar of the black walnut stump-arouse the enthusiasm of the buyers by announcing that a certain three-year-old had as its sire the *Immortal Cunctator* and that its dam was the peerless *Swift Perdition*. Year after year he dwelt there, contented in drinking the limestone water of his hillside spring with his foals and his fillies; drinking at his table the unskimmed milk of his Durham dairy; and drinking indoors and outdoors the waterproof beverage of a four-seasons philosophic decanter. The decanter resembled the limestone spring in this at least: that it could never rise higher than being full and could never be baled dry.

In the vernal season, as sole proprietor of all this teeming rural bliss, he sat on the top rail of a fence and witnessed the manufacture of the hippic generations; in summer sat on the top rail of another fence and saw his colts trained; in autumn in the judges' stand sat with a finger on his watch and saw them win; in winter, passing into a state of partial hibernation over the study of pedigrees, his fingers plunged deep in his beard, with comfortable mumblings and fumblings that bore their analogy to a bear's brumal licking of its paws.

A veritable Roman poet Horace of a man, with yearlings as his odes-and with a few mules for satires.

Surely possessed of some excellent Epicurean philosophy of his own in that he could live so long in a wretched world and escape all wretchedness. If storms broke over his head, he insisted that the weather just then was especially fine; if trouble knocked at the door, he announced with regret from the inside that the door was locked. Is there any wonder that, nobody though he insisted upon being, his appearance in public always attracted a crowd? For the inhabitants of this world are always looking for one happy inhabitant. His acquaintances hurried to him as they would break into a playful run for a barrel of lemonade at a woodland picnic when they needed to be cooled; or as they waited around a kettle of burgroo at a barbecue in autumn when they wished to be warmed. Hot or cold, they felt their need to be sprayed as to their unquiet passions by his streaming benevolence.

Always that benevolence. On two distinct occasions he had placidly reduced by one the entire meritorious population of central Kentucky; and then with a clear countenance, had presented himself at the bar of justice to be cleared. Upon his technical acquittal, the judge had casually said that no matter how guilty he was, it would have been a much fouler crime to hang a citizen with so innocent an expression; that the habitual look of innocence was of more value in a homicidal community than a verdict of guilty for two fits of distemper!

If the world should last until Kentucky passes out of history into the classic and the mythological; if Daniel Boone and the Wilderness Road should become Orion and the Milky Way; if the capture of Betsy Calloway should become the rape of Lucrece; if the two gigantic Indian fighters, the Poe brothers, should establish their claim to the authorship of those Poems and Tales which even in our own time are beginning to fall away from a mythical personage, —hardly more than an emanation of darkness, perhaps this unique Kentucky gentleman who insisted upon being no one at all will exhibit his beaming face in the heavens of those ages as Charioteer to the Horses of the Sun.

The sole warrant for here disturbing his light repose under his patchwork of turf is that he had taken to his hearthstone and heart an orphan nephew, whose destiny it was to be profoundly influenced by the environment of heart and hearthstone: by this breeding of horses, by the method of training them; by that serene outlook upon the world and that gayety of nature which attracted happiness to it as naturally as the martin box in the yard drew the martins. Possibly even more influenced in the earlier years around that fireside where there was no women, no mother, no father, either; nor parent out of doors save the motherhood of the near earth and the fatherhood of the distant sky.

From the day when he arrived on that stock farm its influences began their work upon him and kept it up during years when he was not aware. But in his own memory the first event in the long series of events-the first scene of all the scenes that made his Progress-occurred when he was about fifteen years old. As the middle-aged man, sitting in his library that morning with the Book of the Years before him, reviewed his life, his memory went straight back to that event and stopped there as though it were the beginning. Of course it was not the beginning; of course he could not himself have known where the beginning was or what it was; but he did what we all do as we look back toward childhood and try to open a road as far as memory will reach, —we begin somewhere, and the doctor began with his fifteenth year-as the first scene of his Progress. But let that scene be painted not as the doctor saw it: more nearly as it was: he was too young to know all that it contained.

It was a balmy Saturday afternoon of early summer; and uncle and nephew were out in the yard of the white and lemon-colored manor house, enjoying the shade of some blossoming locust trees. The uncle was sitting in a yellow cane-bottom chair; and he had on a yellow nankeen waistcoat and trousers; so that the chair looked like an overgrown architectural harmony attached to his dorsal raiment; and he had on a pleated bosom shirt which had been polished by his negro laundress with iron and paraffine until it looked like a cake of winter ice marked off to be cut in slices. In the top button-hole was a cluster diamond pin which represented almost a star-system; and about his throat was tied a magenta cravat: that was the day for solferinos and magentas and Madeira wine. But the neck of the wearer of the cravat was itself turning to a gouty magenta; so that the ribbon, while appropriately selected, was as a color-sign superfluous. On the grass beside him lay his black alpaca coat and panama hat and gold-headed cane and red silk handkerchief and a piece of dry wood admirable for whittling.

He had been to a colt show that morning several miles across the country in a neighborhood where there was some turbulence; not the turbulence of the colts; and he had reached home just before dinner-glad to get there without turbulence; and the dinner had been good, and now he was experiencing that comfortable expansion of girth which turns even a pessimist toward optimism; that streaming benevolence of his countenance never streamed to better advantage.

He was reading his Saturday weekly newspaper, an entire page of which showed that this was a great thoroughbred breeding-region of the world. At the distance of several yards you could have inferred as much by the character of the advertisements, each of which was headed by the little black wood-cut of a stallion. The page was blackened by this wood-cut as it repeated itself up and down, column after column. Whether the stallion were sorrel or roan or bay or chestnut or black-one wood-cut stood for all. There was one other wood-cut for jacks-all jacks.

In the same way one little wood-cut in an earlier generation had been used to stand for runaway slaves: a negro with a stick swung across his shoulder and with a bundle dangling from the stick down his fugitive back; one wood-cut for all slaves. If you saw between the legs of the figure, it was a man; if you did not-it was the other figure of man's fate in slavery.

The turfman read every item of his newspaper, having first with a due sense of proportion cast his eye on the advertisement of his own stud.

The nephew was lying on the grass near by, wearing a kind of dove-colored suit; so that from a distance he might have been taken for a huge mound of vegetable mould; he having just awakened from a nap: a heavy, rank, insolent, human cub with his powers half pent up and half unfolded, except a fully developed insolence toward all things and people except his uncle, himself, and his friend, Fred Ousley. He rolled drowsily about on the soft turf, waiting to take his turn at the newspaper: it was the only thing he read: otherwise he was too busy reading the things of life on the farm. Once he stretched himself on his back, looking upward for anything and everything in sight. The light breeze swung the boughs of the locust, now heavily draped with blossoms; and soon his eyes began to follow what looked like a flame darting in and out amid the snowy cascades of bloom —a flame that was vocal and that dropped down upon his ear crimson petals of song-the Baltimore oriole.

He liked all birds but three; and presently one of those that he disliked appeared in a fork of a locust and darted at the oriole, driving it away and then returning to the fork-the blue-jay. His hatred of this bird dated from the time when one of the negroes had told him that no blue-jays could be seen at twelve o'clock on Friday-all having gone to carry brimstone to the lower regions. After that he and Fred Ousley had made a point of trying to kill jays early Friday morning: a fatally shied stone would cut off to a dead certainty just so much of that supply of brimstone. He hated them even more on Saturday, when he thought of them as having returned. The one in the fork now was looking down at him, and, with a great mockery of bowing, called out his *Fiddle-Fiddle-Fiddle*: it was his way of saying: "You'll get there: and there will be brimstone, sonny!"

Of course he believed none of this legend; but suggestions live on in the mind even though they do not root themselves in faith; and memory also has its power to make us like and dislike. Presently, as he lay there stretched on the grass and near the edge of the shade, another ill-omened bird came sailing cloud-high across the blue firmament; and having taken notice of him, —a motionless form on the earth below, —it turned back and began to circle about him. That was another bird he hated. When a child he asked about it, and had been told that it removed all disagreeable things from the farms. He thought it a very kind, very self-sacrificing and industrious bird to do so. And he conceived the whole species of them as a procession of wheelbarrows operated across the sky by means of wings and tails. Afterwards, when his views grew less hazy on natural history, he lowered his opinion of the disinterested buzzard.

The third bird on which had fallen his resentment was the rain-crow: earlier in his childhood it had been told him that when the clacking wail of this songster was heard on the stillness of a summer day, a storm was coming. And he had seen storms enough on that very farm-tornadoes that cut a path through the woods as a reaper cuts his way across the wheat-field. But he saw no rain-crow to-day; you look for them in August when they haunt the cool shade-trees of lawns.

Altogether these three birds made with one another a rather formidable combination for a boy living on a farm: the one brought on storms that threatened life; the second gladly presided at your obsequies, if the opportunity were given; and the third was pleased to accompany you to the infernal regions with the necessary fuel. The arrangement seemed about perfect; apparently they had overlooked nothing of value.

Thus he had not escaped that vast romance of Nature which brooded more thickly over Kentucky country life in those days than now: a romance of superstitions and legends about bird life and animal life and tree life, that extended even to Nature's chemicals; for was there not brimstone with its story? As far back as he could remember he had been made familiar with the idea-rather terrible in its way-that there was a variety of Biblical horse which breathed brimstone. All alone one day he had made a somewhat cautious personal examination of the paddocks and stalls; and was relieved to discover that his uncle's horses breathed out only what they breathed in-Kentucky air. He felt glad that they were not of the breed of those Biblical chargers.

But then there was brimstone in reserve for a large portion of the human family; and with a perverse mocking deviltry he pushed his inquiry in this direction still farther. Without the knowledge of any one he had wasted at a drugstore in town his brightest dime for a package of the avenging substance; and at home the following day he had scraped chips together at the woodpile and started a blaze and poured the brimstone in. Actually he had a sample of hell fire in operation there behind the woodpile! There was no question that brimstone knew how to burn: it seemed well adapted for its purpose. He did not take Fred Ousley into his confidence in this experiment: the possibilities were a little too personal even for friendship!

All this reveals a trait in him which lay deeper than child's-play —a susceptibility to suggestion. Even while he amused himself as a child with the shams and superstitions about nature, these lived on in his mind as part of its furnishings. Alas, that this should be true for all of us-that we cannot forget the things we do not believe in. To the end of our lives our thoughts have to move amid the obstructions and rubbish of the useless and the laughable. The salon of our inner dwelling is largely filled with old furniture which we decline to sit in, but are obliged to look at, and are powerless to remove; and which fills the favorite recesses where we should like to arrange the new.

There they were, then, that Saturday afternoon: the uncle with his newspaper and the nephew at that moment with his group of evil birds.

There was an interruption. Around the yard with its velvet turf and blooming shrubs and vines and flowers, that filled the air with fragrance, was a plank fence newly whitewashed. All the fences of the farm had been newly whitewashed; and they ran hither and thither across the emerald of the landscape like structures of white marble. Through the gate of the yard fence which was heard to shut behind him there now advanced toward uncle and nephew a neighbor of theirs, the minister of the country church, himself a bluegrass farmer. He was one of the many who liked to seek the company of the untroubled turfman. The two were good neighbors and great friends. The minister came oftenest for a visit on Saturday afternoons, as if he wished to touch at this harbor of a quiet life while passing from the earthly fields of the week to the Sabbath's holy land.

At the sound of the latch the uncle lifted his eyes from his newspaper.

"Bring a chair, Downs, will you?" he said in a cordial undertone; and soon there was a fine group of rural humanity under the blossoming locusts: the two men talking, and the boy, now that his turn had come at last, lying on the grass absorbed in the newspaper.

The men were characters of broad plain speech, much like English squires of two centuries earlier: not ladylike men: Chaucer might have been pleased to make one of their group and listen, and turn them afterwards into fine old English tales; Hogarth might have craved the privilege to sit near and observe and paint; and a certain Sir John Falstaff might have been at home with them-in the absence of the "Merry Wives."

There was another interruption. Around the corner of the manor house a young servant advanced, bearing a waiter with two deep glasses well filled: at the bottom the drink was golden; it was green and snow-white at the top: a little view of icebergs with pine trees growing on them.

The servant smiled and approached with embarrassment, having discovered a guest; and in a lowered tone she offered to the master of the house apologies for not bringing three.

"This is yours, Aleck," said the host, holding out one glass to the minister. "This is for you, Downs. Now, Melissa, make me one, will you?"

"None for me," said the minister.

"Then never mind, Melissa. But wait-lemonade?"

"Yes; lemonade. It is the very thing."

"As it is or as it might be?"

"As it is."

"Lemonade without the decanter, Melissa."

While the servant was in the house, the uncle and the nephew waited with their glasses untouched.

The turfman was very happy-happy in his guest, in his nephew, in himself, in everything: his mind overflowed with his quaint playfulness; and when he talked, you were loath to interrupt him.

"Aleck," he said, rattling the ice in his julep, "don't you suppose that when we get to heaven, nothing will make us happier there than remembering the good times we had in this world? so if you want to be happy there, be happy here. *This* is one of the pleasures that I expect to carry in memory if I am ever transformed into a male seraph. But I may not have to remember. If there is any provision made for the thirst of the Kentucky redeemed, do you know what I think will be the reward of all central Kentucky male angels? From under the great white throne there will trickle an ice-cold stream of this, ready-made —and I shouldn't wonder if there were a Kentuckian under the throne making it. The Kentucky delegation would be camped somewhere near, though there will be two delegations, of course, because they will divide on politics. And don't you fear that there will not be others hastening to the banks of that stream! It is too late to look for young Moses in the bulrushes; but I shouldn't wonder if the whole ransomed universe discovered old Moses in the mint."

"*Which mint?*" said the minister, who kept his worldly wits about him.

"Aleck," replied the turfman, "I leave it to you whether that is not too flippant a remark with which to close a gentleman's solemn discourse."

The lemonade was served.

"Is yours sour enough, Aleck?"

The visitor found it to his taste.

"Is yours sweet enough, Downs?"

This hurt Downs' feelings: it implied that he was not old enough to like things sour. He replied surlily that his might have been stronger.

The servant, watching from inside a window, judged by the angle at which the glasses were tilted that they were empty: she returned and asked whether she should bring 'one more all around.'

"More lemonade, Aleck?"

"Thank you, no more for me-but it was good, better than yours."

"Another for you, Downs?"

Downs thought that he would not have another just for the moment: the servant disappeared.

The nephew returned to his paper. The turfman took from the turf a piece of whittling wood, split it, and handed the larger piece to the minister. The minister produced his penknife and began to whittle. In those days a countryman who did not carry his penknife with a big blade well sharpened for whittling as he talked with his neighbor stood outside the manners and customs of a simple cheerful land. And now the two friends were ready to enjoy their afternoon-the vicar of souls and the vicar of the stables.

The minister began to speak of his troubles-with that strange leaning we all have to let our confidences fall upon people who are not too good: the vicar of the stables was not too good to be sympathetic. It was all summed up in one sentence-discouragement about his growing boys. From the beginnings of their lives he had tried to teach them the things they were not to do; and all their lives they had seemed bent on doing those things. He felt disheartened as the boys grew older and their waywardness increased. *What not to do* —morning and night *what not to do.* Yet they were always doing it.

Out under the trees the peaceful happy sounds of summer life in the yard came to the ears of the minister as nature's chorus of happiness and indifference. The breeder of thorough-breds, as his friend grew silent, laughed with his peaceful nature, and remarked with respect and gentleness: —

"I never train my colts in that way."

"My sons are not colts," said the minister, laughing. "Nor young jackasses!"

"Yes, I know they are not colts; but I doubt whether their difference makes any difference in the training of the two species of animal."

After a pause which was filled with little sounds made by the industrious penknives, the master of the stables went into the matter for the pleasure of it: —

"You tell me that you have tried a method of training and that it is a failure. I don't wonder: any training would be a failure that made it the chief business in life of any creature-human or brute-to fix its mind upon what it is *not* to do. You say you are always warning your boys; that you fill their minds with cautions; that you arouse their imagination with pictures of forbidden things; make them look at life as a check, a halter, a blind bridle. So far as I can discover, you have prepared a list of the evil traits of humanity and required your boys to memorize these: and then you tell them to beware. Is that it?"

"That is exactly it."

The youth lying on the grass laid aside his newspaper and began to listen. The two men welcomed his attention. The minister always found it difficult to speak without a congregation-part of which must be sinners: here was an occasion for outdoor preaching. The turfman probably welcomed this chance to get before the youth in an indirect way certain suggestions which he relied upon for his: —

"Well, that is where your training and my training differ," he resumed. "I never assemble my colts at the barn door-that is, I would not if I could-and recite to them the vicious traits of the wild horse and require them to memorize those traits and think about them unceasingly, but never to imitate them. Speaking of jacks, Aleck, you know our neighbor stands a jack. And he would not if he could compel his jack to make a study of the peculiarities of Balaam's ass. But you compel your boys to make a study of Balaam and his tribes. You teach them the failings of mankind as they revealed themselves in an age of primitive transgression. I say I never try to train a horse that way. On the contrary I try to let all the ancestral memories slumber, and I take all the ancestral powers and develop them for modern uses. Why, listen. We know that a horse's teeth were once useful as a weapon to bite its enemies. Now I try to give it the notion that its teeth are only useful in feeding. You know that its hoofs were used to strike its enemies: it stood on its forefeet and kicked in the rear; it stood on its hind feet and pawed in front. You know that the horse is timid, it is born timid, dies timid; but had it not been timid, it would have been exterminated: its speed was one of its means of survival: if it could not conquer, it had to flee and the sentinel of its safety was its fear; it was the most valuable trait it had; this ancestral trait has not yet been outlived; don't despise the horse for it. But now I try to teach a horse that feet and legs and speed are to serve another instinct-the instinct to win in the new maddened courage of the race-course. And I never allow the horse to believe that it has such a thing as an enemy. He is not to fear life, but to trust life. I teach him that man is not his old hereditary enemy, but his friend-and his master. I would not suggest to a horse any of its latent bad traits. I never prohibit its doing anything. I never try to teach it what not to do, but only what to do. And so I have good colts, and you have-but excuse me!"

The minister stood up and brushed the shavings from his lap and legs; then as he took his seat he covered his side of the discussion with one breath: —

"I hold to the old teaching-good from the foundation of the world-that the old must tell the young what not to do."

"Aleck," replied the vicar of the stables with his quaint sunniness, "don't you know that no human being can teach any living thing-man or beast or bird or fish or flea —*not* to do a thing? you can only teach *to do*. If there is a God of this universe, He is a God of doing. You can no more teach 'a not' than you can teach 'a nothing.' Now try to teach one of your sons nothing! This world has never taught, and will never teach, a prohibition, because a prohibition is a nothing; it has never taught anything but the will and desire to do: that is the root of the matter. Do you suppose I try to keep one of my cows from kicking over the bucket of milk by tying her hind legs? I go to the other end of the beast and do something for her brain so that when she feels the instinct to kick which is her right, what I have taught her will compel her to waive her right and to keep her feet on the ground. That is all there is of it."

They were hearty and good-humored in their talk, and the minister did not budge: but the boy listened only to his uncle.

"Do you remember, Aleck, when you and I were in the school over yonder and one morning old Bowles issued a new order that none of us boys was to ask for a drink between little recess and big recess? Now none of us drank at that hour; but the day after the order was issued, every boy wanted a drink, and demanded a drink, and got a drink. It was thirst for principle. Every boy knew it was his right to drink whenever he was thirsty-and even when he was not thirsty; and he disobeyed orders to assert that right. And if old Bowles had not lowered his authority before that advancing right, there would not have been any old Bowles. There is one thing greater than any man's authority, and that is any man's right. Isn't that the United States? Wasn't that Kentucky country school-house the United States? And don't you know, Aleck, that as soon as a thing is forbidden, human nature investigates the command to see whether it puts forth an infringement of its liberties? Don't you *know*, Aleck, that the disobedience of children may be one of their natural rights?"

At this point the uncle turned unexpectedly toward his nephew: —

"Does this bore you, Downs?"

Downs remarked pointedly that half of it bored him: he made it perfectly clear which was the objectionable half.

The uncle did not notice the discourtesy to his guest, but continued his amiable observation: —

"To me it all leads up to this-and now the road turns away from colts to the road you and I walk in as men. It leads up to this: the difference between failure and transgression. Command to do; and the worst result can only be failure. Command not to do; and the worst result is transgression. Now we all live on partial failure: it is the beginning of effort and the incentive to effort. We try and fail; with more will and strength and experience we wipe out the failure and stand beyond it. Long afterwards men look back and laugh at their failures, love them because they are the measure of what they were and of what they have become. It is our life, the glory of more strength, the triumph of will and determination. It is the crowning victory of the world. And it is the road that leads upward.

"But transgression! No transgression ever develops life; it is so much death. You can't wrest victory out of transgression: it's a thing by itself —a final defeat. And what has been defeated is your last safeguard-your will. Every transgression helps to kill the will. It weakens, discourages, humiliates, stings, poisons. The road of transgression is downward."

He stood up, and his guest with him. As he lifted his alpaca coat from the grass and put it on, there was left lying his bowie-knife, and he put that on. It was the bowie-knife age.

"Will you come with us, Downs?"

Downs thought he would now read the newspaper.

"Where is Fred Ousley?" asked the minister of him, knowing that the two boys were inseparable.

"He has gone to a picnic."

"Why didn't you go to the picnic?"

"I wasn't invited: it's his cousins'."

"And haven't you any cousins who give picnics?"

"I don't like my cousins: I hate my cousins: Fred hates *his* cousins: it's a girl that goes *with* his cousins."

"And what about a girl with your cousins?"

"Well, while you're talking, what about your sons and their cousins? We're running this farm very well, and we're all pleased. From what I have been hearing, it's more than can be said about yours."

The minister laughed good-naturedly at this rudeness as the two friends walked away; but the vicar of the stables observed mildly: —

"You gave him the wrong kind of suggestion, Aleck. It wasn't in your words exactly; I don't know where it was; but I felt it and he felt it: somehow you challenged him to employ his manly art of self-defence; and part of that art is to attack. But never mind about Downs. Now come to the stable: I am going to show you a young thoroughbred there that has never had a disagreeable suggestion made to him: he thinks this farm paradise. And the five great things I tried to teach him are: to develop his will, to develop his speed, to develop his endurance and perseverance, to develop his pride, and to develop his affection: he is a masterpiece."

In the green yard that summer afternoon, under the white locust blossoms and with the fragrance of rose and honeysuckle and lilac all about him, the youth lay on the grass beside the newspaper-which he forgot. A new world of thinking had been disclosed to him. And he made one special discovery: that as far as memory could reach his uncle had never told him not to do anything: always it had been to do-never not to do.

And he was a good deal impressed with the difference between failure and transgression. He did not at all like that idea of transgression; but he thought he should like to try failure for a while; then he could call on more strength, tighten his will, develop more fighting power. He rather welcomed that combat with failure which would end in success.

He wished Fred were there. It was Saturday he came to stay all night; and the two were getting old enough to talk about their futures and at what ages each would marry. They described the desirable type of woman; and sometimes exchanged descriptions.

And then suddenly he rolled over the grass convulsed with laughter: his uncle was raising him as a thoroughbred colt. He approved of the training, but somehow he did not feel complimented by the classification. Fred would have to hear that-that he was being trained as for a race-course.

The next morning he was sitting in church; and the minister read the Commandments.

Hitherto he had always listened to them as the whole congregation apparently listened: as to a noise from the pulpit that drew near, lasted for a while, and then rumbled on-without being meant for any one. But this morning he scrutinized each Commandment with new thoughtfulness-and with a new resentfulness also; and when a certain one was reached he made a discovery that it applied to men only: "Thou shalt not covet thy neighbor's wife."

Why should not wives be commanded not to covet their neighbors' husbands? he wondered. Why was the other half of the Commandment suppressed? Moses must have been a very polite man! Perhaps there was more involved than courtesy: otherwise he might have found life more tolerable among the Egyptians: he might have been forced to make the return trip across the Red Sea when the waters were inconveniently deep. Those Jewesses of the Wandering might have seen to it that he was not to have the pleasure of dying so mysteriously on Nebo's lonely mountain: his sepulchre would have been marked-and well marked.

He sat there in the corner of the church, and plied his insolent satire. Fred Ousley must hear about the second discovery also-the Commandment for men only.

Then three years passed and he was eighteen; and from fifteen to eighteen is a long time in youth's life; things are much worse or things are much better.

It was one rainy September night after supper, and he and his uncle were sitting on opposite sides of the deep fireplace.

Some logs blazed comfortably, and awoke in both man and youth the thoughtfulness which lays such a silence upon us with the kindling of the earliest Autumn fires. Talk between them was never forced. It came, it went: they were at perfect ease with one another in their comradeship. The man's long thoughts went backward; the youth's long thoughts went forward. The man was smoking, at intervals serenely drawing his amber-hued meerschaum from under his thick mustache. The youth was not smoking-he was waiting to be a man. Once his uncle had remarked: "Tobacco is for men if they wish tobacco, and for pioneer old ladies if they must have their pipes. Begin to smoke after you are a man, Downs. Cigars for boys are as bad as cigars would be for old ladies."

The way in which this had been put rather captured the youth's fancy: he was determined to have every inward and outward sign of being a man: now he was waiting for the cigar.

He had been hunting with Fred Ousley that afternoon, and just before dark had come in with a good bag of birds. A drizzle of rain had overtaken him in the fields and dampened his clothing. The truth is that he and Ousley had lingered over their good-by; Fred was off for college. Supper was over when he reached the house, and he had merely washed his hands and gone in to supper as he was, eating alone; and now as he sat gazing into the fire, his boots and his hunting-trousers and his dark blue flannel shirt began to steam. He was too much a youth to mind wet garments.

The man on the opposite side sent secret glances across at him: they were full of pride, of a man's idolatry of a scion of his own blood. He was thinking of the blood of that family-blood never to be forced or hurried: death rather than being commanded: rage at being ordered: mingled of Scotch and Irish and Anglo-Saxon —with the Kentucky wildness and insolence added. Blood that often wallowed in the old mires of humanity; then later in life by a process of unfolding began to set its course toward the virtues of the world and ultimately stood where it filled lower men with awe.

September was the month for the opening of schools and colleges. The boy's education had been difficult and desultory. First he had gone to the neighborhood school, then to a boys' select school, then to a military school, then to a college. Usually he quit and came home. Once he had joined his uncle in another State at the Autumn meeting of a racing association-had merely walked up to him on the grounds, eating purple grapes out of a paper bag and with his linen trousers pockets bulging with ripe peaches.

"Well, Downs," his uncle observed by way of greeting him, as though he had reappeared round a corner.

"Who won the last race?" inquired the boy as though he had been absent ten minutes.

Now out of the silence of the rainy September night and out of the thoughtfulness of the fire, the imperious splendid dark glowing young animal steaming in his boots and flannel suddenly looked across and spoke: —

"If I am ever going to do anything, it is about time I began."

The philosopher on the other side of the fire grew wary; he had given the blood time, and now the blood was mounting to the brain.

"It is time, if you think it is time."

"One thing I am not going to do," said the arbiter of his fate, as if he were drawing a surprise from the depths of his nature and were offering it to his uncle; if possible, without discourtesy, but certainly without discussion —"one thing I am not going to do; I am not going to breed horses."

The fire crackled, and no other sound disturbed the stillness.

"Some one else will breed them," replied the vicar of the stables, with quietness: the sun always seemed to remain on his face after it had gone down. "They will be bred by some one else. The breeding of horses in the world will not be stopped because some one does not wish to breed them. It will come to the same thing in the end. Even if it does not come to the same thing, it will come to something different. No matter, either way."

The young hunter had unbuttoned one of his shirt sleeves and bared his arm above the elbow; and he now stroked his forearm as he bent it backward over the biceps and suddenly struck out at the air as though he would knock the head off of an idea.

"My notion is this: I don't want to stand still and let my horse do the running. If I have a horse, I want it to stand still and let me do the running. If there is any excitement for either of us, I want the excitement. I don't care *to own* an animal that wins a race: I want *to be* the animal that wins a race."

"Then be the animal that wins the race! The horse will win his races: he will take care of himself: win your race."

"I intend to win my race."

There was silence for a while.

"As it is not to be horses, then, I have been thinking of other things I might do."

"Keep on thinking."

"You might help me to think."

"I am ready to think with you; you can only think for yourself."

"What about going into the army?"

"You just said you wanted excitement. There is no excitement in the army unless there is war. We have just passed through one war, and I don't think either of us will live to see another. Still, if you wish, I can get you to West Point. Or, if you prefer the navy, I can get you to Annapolis."

"No Annapolis for me! I wouldn't live on anything that I couldn't walk about on and sit down on and roll over on. No water for me. I'll take land all round me in every direction. I guess I'll leave the sea to the Apostle Peter. Life on land and death on land for me. Hard showers and streams and ponds and springs-that will do for water. No Annapolis, thank you!"

"West Point, then."

"If I went into the army, wouldn't I have to leave the farm here?"

"You'd have to leave the farm here unless the Government would quarter some troops here for your accommodation. In case of war, you might arrange with the enemy to come to Kentucky and attack you where you would be comfortable."

The future officer of his country did not smile at this: his manner seemed to indicate that such a concession might not be so absurd. He did not budge from his position: —

"I'd rather do something that would let me live here."

"You could live here and study law: some of the greatest members of the Kentucky bar have been farmers. You could live here and practise law in the country seat."

"Suppose I studied law and then some day I were called to the Supreme Bench: wouldn't that take me away?"

"It might take you away unless the Supreme Court would get down from its Bench and come and sit on your bench-always to accommodate you."

"I don't know about law: I'll have to think: law *does* make you think!"

"There is the pulpit: some of the greatest Kentucky divines have been bluegrass farmers-though I've always wished that they wouldn't call themselves divines. It's more than Christ did!"

"The pulpit! And then all my life I'd be thinking of other people's faults and failings. A fine time I'd have, trying to chase my friends to hell."

The next suggestion followed in due order.

"There's Oratory; some of the great Kentucky orators have been bluegrass farmers. There is Southern Oratory."

"Oratory-where would I get my gas?"

"Manufacture it. It always has to be manufactured. The consumer always manufactures."

"If I went in for oratory, you *know* I'd come out in Congress; you know they always do: then no farm for me again."

"That is, unless-you know, Congress might adjourn and hold its sessions-that same idea-to accommodate you —!"

"I'd like to be a soldier and I'd like to be a farmer, if I could get the two professions together."

"They went together regularly in pioneer Kentucky. The soldiers were farmers and the farmers were soldiers."

"And then if I could be a doctor. That's what I'd like best. To be a soldier and a farmer and a doctor."

"Men were all three in pioneer Kentucky. During the period of Indian wars the Kentucky farmer and soldier, who was the border scout, was also sometimes the scout of Æsculapius."

"Æsculapius-who was he? Trotter, runner, or pacer?"

"He set the pace: you might call him a pacer."

What a sense of deep peace and security and privacy there was in the two being thus free to talk together of life and the world-in that womanless house! No woman sitting beside the fire to interject herself and pull things her way; or to sit by without a sign-and pull things her way afterwards-without a sign.

The physical comfort of the night, and the rain, and the snug hearth awoke a desire for more confidences.

"Tell me about the medical schools when you were a student. Not about the professors. I don't want to hear anything about the professors. You wouldn't know anything about *them*, anyhow: no student ever does. But what were the students up to among themselves at nights? The wild ones. I don't want to hear anything about the goody-goody ones. Tell me about the devils-the worst of the devils."

The medical schools of those days, as members of the profession yet living can testify if they would, had their stories of student life that make good stories when recited around the fireside with September rain on the roof. The former graduate and non-practitioner was not averse seemingly to reminiscence. Forthwith he entered upon some chronicles and pursued them with that soft, level voice of either betting with you or baptizing you-the voice of gambling in this world or of gambling for the next.

As the recitals wound along their channels, the listener's enthusiasm became stirred: by degrees it took on a kindling that was like a wild leaping flame of joy.

"But there always has to be a leader," he said, as though forecasting for himself a place of such splendid prominence. "There has to be a leader, a head."

"I was the head."

The young hunter on the opposite side of the fireplace suddenly threw up his arms and rolled out of his chair and lay on the floor as though he had received a charge of buckshot in one ear. At last, gathering himself up on the floor, he gazed at the tranquil amber pipe and tranquil piper: —

"*You!*"

There was a mild wave of the hand by the historian of the night, much as one puts aside a faded wreath, deprecating being crowned with it a second time.

"Another shock like that——!" and the searcher for a profession climbed with difficulty into his chair again. For a while there was satisfied silence, and now things took on a graver character: —

"Somehow I feel," said the younger of the men, "that there have been great men all about here. I don't see any now; but I have a feeling that they have been here-great men. I feel them behind me-all kinds of great men. It is like the licks where we now find the footprints and the bones of big game, larger animals that have vanished. There are the bones of greater men in Kentucky: I feel their lives behind me."

"They *are* behind you: the earth is rank with them. You need not look anywhere else for examples. I don't know how far you got in your Homer at school before you were tired of it; but there is the *Iliad* of Kentucky: I am glad you have begun to read *that*!"

The rain on the shingles and in the gutters began to sound like music. The two men alone there in their talk about life, not a woman near, a kind of ragged sublimity.

"To be a soldier and to be a farmer-if I could get those two professions together," persisted the youth.

"In times of peace there is only one profession that furnishes the active soldier: and that is the profession of medicine. It is the physician and the surgeon that the military virtues rest on; and the martial traits when there is no war. It is these men that bring those virtues and those traits undiminished from one war to the next war. There is no kind of manhood in the soldier, the fighting man, that is not in the fighting physician and fighting surgeon-fighting against disease. There is nothing that has to be changed in these two when war breaks out or when peace comes: their constant service fits them for either. In times of peace the only warlike type of man actively engaged in human life is the doctor and surgeon. Did you ever think of that?" said the older man, persuasively.

The silence in the room grew deeper.

"Tell me about the professions in the War: what did they do about it; how did they act?"

"The professions divided: some going with North, some going with South; fighting on each side, fighting one another. The ministry dividing most bitterly and sending up their prayers on each side for the destruction of the other-to the same God. All except one: the profession of medicine remained indivisible. For that is the profession which has but a single ideal, a single duty, a single work, and but one patient-Man."

The silence had become too deep for words.

The young hunter quietly got up and lit his candle and squared himself in the middle of the floor, pale with the sacred fire of a youth's ideal.

"I am going to be a Kentucky country doctor. Good night!" He strode heavily out of the room, and his stride on the stairway sounded like an upward march toward future glory.

The man at the fire listened. Usually when the youth had reached his room above and set his candle on his stand beside his bed, he undressed there as with one double motion of shucking an ear of corn: half to right and half to left; and then the ear stood forth bared in its glistening whiteness and rounded out to perfect form with clean vitality. But now for a long time he heard a walking back and forth, a solemn tread: life's march had begun in earnest.

He rose from his chair and tapped the ash out of his meerschaum. Through force of habit and old association with the race-course he looked at his timepiece.

"I win that race in good time," he said. "That colt was hard to manage, obstreperous and balky."

It had always been his secret wish that his nephew would enter the profession that he himself had spurned. Perhaps no man ever ceases to have some fondness for the profession he has declined, as perhaps a woman will to the last send some kind thoughts toward the man she has rejected.

After winning a race, he always poured out a libation; and he went to his sideboard now and poured out a libation sixteen years old.

And he did not pour it on the ground.

And now eight years followed, during which the youth Downs Birney became young Dr. Birney —a very great stage of actual progress. Seven away from Kentucky, and one there since his return. Of those seven, five in New York for a degree; and two in Europe-in Berlin, in Vienna-for more lectures, more hospital work, another degree. At the end of the second he returned incredibly developed to Kentucky, to the manor house and the stock farm; and to the uncle to whom these years had furnished abundance of means whereby to get the best of all that was wisely to be gotten: an affectionate abundance, no overfond super-abundance, no sentimentality: merely a quiet Kentucky sun throwing the energy of its rays along that young life-track —hanging out a purse of gold at each quarter-stretch, to be snatched as the thoroughbred passed.

A return home then to a neighborhood of kinships and friendships and to the uphill work which could so easily become downhill sliding-the practice of medicine among a people where during these absences he had been remembered, if remembered at all, as the wildest youth in the country. When it had been learned what profession he had chosen, the prediction had been made that within a year Downs would reduce the mortality of the neighborhood to normal-one to every inhabitant!

But at the end of this first year of undertaking to convert ridicule into acceptance of himself as a stable health officer and confidential health guardian, he was able to say that he had made a good start: neighbors have long memories about a budding physician's first cases-when he fails. Young Dr. Birney had not failed, because none of his cases had been important: when there was danger, it was considered safe to avoid the doctor: the only way in which he could have lost a patient would have been to murder one! Thus he had entered auspiciously upon the long art and science of securing patients. But he had secured no wife! And he greatly preferred one impossible wife to all possible patients. That problem meantime had been pressing him sorely.

The womanless house in which he had been reared and his boyhood on a stock farm had rendered him rather shy of girls and kept him much apart from the society of the neighborhood. Nevertheless even in Europe before his return-with the certainty of marriage before him-he had recalled two or three juvenile perturbations, and he had resolved upon arrival to follow these clues and ascertain what changes seven years had wrought in them. There was no difficulty in following the clues a few weeks after getting back to Kentucky: they led in each case to the door of a growing young family: and out of these households he thereupon began to receive calls for his services to sick children: all the perturbations had become volcanoes, and were now on their way to become extinct craters.

So he was clueless. He must make his own clues and then follow. Nor could there be any dallying, since he could not hope to succeed in his profession as a young unmarried physician: thus pressure from without equalled pressure from within.

Moreover, he was pleasantly conscious of a general commotion of part of the population toward him with reference to life's romance. The girls of that race and land were much too healthy and normally imaginative not to feel the impact of the arrival of a young doctor-who was going to ask one of them to marry him. As to those seven years of his in New York and Europe, he could discover only one mind in them: they deplored his absence not because they had missed *him*, but because he had missed *them*: it was no gain to have been in New York and Berlin and Vienna if you lost Kentucky! He gradually acquired the feeling that if in addition to the misfortune of having been absent for several years, the calamity had been his of having been born abroad, it would not have been permitted him to plough corn.

But while they could not abet him in the error of thinking that he had returned a cosmopolitan, bringing high prestige, instantly they showed general excitement that he-one of themselves-was at home again in search of a wife. He had arrived like a starving bee released in a ripe vineyard; and for a while he could only whirl about, distracted by indecision as to what cluster of grapes he should settle on: not that the grapes did not have something to say as to the privilege of alighting. After the bee had selected the bunch, the bunch selected the bee. A vineyard ripe to be gathered-and being gathered! Every month or so a vine disappeared-claimed for Love's vintage-stored away in Love's cellar.

They were everywhere! As he drove widely about the country, the two most abundant characteristics seemed to be unequalled grass and marriageable girls. He met them on turnpikes and lanes-in leafy woods at picnics-at moonlight dances-on velvet lawns-amid the roses of old gardens-and he began humorously to count those who looked available. One passed him on the road one day, and, lifting a corner of the buggy curtain, she peeped back at him: "She will do!" he said. Another swept past him on horseback and looked in the opposite direction. "She will do!" he said. He met two on a shady street of a quiet town under their peach-blow parasols: "They will do!" he said. He saw four on a lawn playing tennis, and watched their vital abandon and tasted their cup: "They will do!" he said. He swept his eyes over a ball-room one night: "They will all do!" he said, and made an end of counting.

Into this world of romance and bride-seeking the doctor launched himself formally under brilliant auspices of earth and sky and people one beautiful afternoon of early summer: it was on the grounds of one of the finest old country places at a lawn party with tennis matches. It was his first appearance as a candidate for life's greater game. A large gallery of onlookers, seated along a trellis of vines and roses, measured him critically as he stepped out on the court: he knew it and he challenged the criticism. In his white flannels; his big bared head covered with curling black hair; his neck half bare in its virile strength; his big grayish blue eyes flashing with glorious health, full of good humor and of deeper warmth; his big half-bared arms strong to hold in love or to lift in pain; the big stub nose of tenacity; the big red mouth that laughing revealed the big thick white teeth, good to tear and grind their way: his twenty-six years of native Kentucky insolence capped with a consciousness of travel and knowledge of his own authority and power-youthful white soldier of the clean, —the neighborhood's evangelist of life and death, —he looked like a good partner for the afternoon or for life. One girl, seeing all this-and more-repeated to herself, she did not know why, Blake's poem on the Tiger.

His partner that afternoon was his hostess —a Kentucky girl just home from her Northern college as a graduate. She too had been away for several years; and they had this in common as the first bond-that they had arrived as comparative strangers and saw their home surroundings from the outside: they spoke of it: it introduced them.

There was tension in the play for this reason; and for others: this first public appearance with so much going on in imagination and sympathy. Too great tension developed as the battle of the racquets went on: so that the doctor's partner, overreaching and twisting, sprained an ankle, and the games ended for them: she was assisted upstairs, and he applied his skill and his treatment.

As he drove home he thought a good deal of his partner: of her proud reserve toward him out of the game and of her inseparable blending of herself with him in the game; her devotion to their common cause; her will not that she should win but that both should win; her unruffled ignoring of a bad play of his or a bad play of her own; the freshened energy of her attack after a reverse; her matter-of-course pleasure when he played well or when she played well; the complete surrender of herself to him for the game-after which instantly there was nothing between them except the courtesy of a hostess. He thought of these traits. And then he recalled her fortitude during the acute suffering with that twisted ankle! How contemptuously she had borne pain!

"That little foot," he said, moved to admiration, "that little foot makes the true footprint of the greater vanished people! She is of the blood of male and female heroes: she knows how to do and she knows how to suffer! Now if I fall in love with her —!" and there surged through him the invitation to do so.

But at the end of his first year the doctor felt that he had made only a general advance toward the long battle-line of Love; he had reconnoitred, but he had not attacked; he had a vast marital receptivity embracing many square miles. He had slid his hands along the nuptial rope, but he could not as yet discover who was waiting beside the bridal knot.

On the other hand, there were two or three cases of wounded on the other side; and if one could have been privileged to stand near, it would have been possible to see Love's ambulances secretly and mournfully moving here and there to the rear. If as much as this could not be said for him, what right would he have had to be practising there-or to be alive anywhere!

And now the winter of that first year had come: it brought an immense stride-in Progress.

It was the twenty-fourth of December. Darkness was beginning to fall on road and woods and fields; and he was driving rapidly home because he was tired and ravenous and because he was thinking of his supper-always that good Kentucky supper. But to-night he would have to eat solitary because some days previous his uncle had gone to New York-gone in his quiet way: announcing the fact one morning and stopping there-his reasons were his own.

About a mile from home the doctor's horse, rushing on through the gathering Christmas twilight, began to overtake a vehicle moving at a stately pace as though its mission involved affairs too elaborate for haste. As he approached from the rear he recognized that it was Frederick Ousley's carriage, returning from his afternoon wedding several miles across the country.

He had never met the girl that his friend was to marry: her home was in another neighborhood, and the demands of this first year upon him had been too many. He had not even had time to go to the wedding. Now he checked his horse in order not to pass the carriage, and at a respectful distance of a few yards constituted himself its happy procession. At the front gate it turned in and rolled through the woods to the house, the windows of which were blazing with candles-bridal lights and the lights of Christmas Eve! He stopped at the gate and followed the progress of it as it intercepted the lights now of one window and now of another as it wound along the drive. Leaning forward with his forearms on his knees and peering from the side-curtain, he saw the front doors thrown open, or knew this by the flood of radiance that issued from the hall; saw the young master of the house walk to the top step of his porch and there turn and wait to receive his bride-in true poetic and royal and manly fashion: wishing her to come to him as he faced her on his threshold; he saw arms outstretched toward her, saw her mount falteringly and give her hands; and saw them walk side by side into the hall: the servants closed in upon them, the doors closed upon the servants.

Christmas Eve-Night of Nativity-Home-Youth-Love-Firelight and Darkness-One another!

As the doctor watched, that vision sank into him as an arrow which had been shot into the air years before and had now hit its mark. He straightened himself abruptly and gave the rein to his horse with a feeling that the shaft stuck in its wound. Then with a vigorous shake of his head he said to himself:—

"Dr. Birney, there is a young man in this buggy who needs your best attention: see that he gets it and gets it quickly."

He found his supper awaiting him: and some intelligence which drove appetite away and drove him away, leaving the supper uneaten: it was a letter from his uncle-one of those tranquil letters:—

"They think they will have to perform an operation on me, but I want your opinion first. I trust your judgment beyond that of any of them, old and experienced as they are: and I should have sought your judgment before coming away if I could have felt sure that it would be needed: unless it were needed, I did not wish you to know. You had better start without losing very much time. They seem to regard the case as urgent and uncertain.

"If anything should happen before you are able to reach me, these few words will be my last.

"You have long since entered, Downs, into possession of part of what you will inherit from me: and that is your acquaintance with the imperfections of my character and the frailties of my life. There has been much in it that even a worse man might regret, but nothing of which any better man could be ashamed. You have always guarded this part of your inheritance as your sacred private personal property. My request is that you will hereafter make as little account of it as possible; I hope you will never be tempted to draw upon it as a valuable fund; and as early as time permits, put the memory of it away to gather its oblivion and its dust.

"You will find that everything of value I possess has been left to you. You think I have loved horses; I have loved nothing but you. I have loved you because you were worthy of it; but I should have loved you if you had not been worthy. The horses meant a good deal to me in life, but they mean nothing in death.

"I believe you will be one more great Kentucky country doctor. And whatever race you may have to run in this world, whether you win or whether you lose, I know it will be a hard, a gallant, struggle: that is all the thoroughbred can ever do. Having delivered over to you everything I own and retaining only the things I cannot will away,—my judgment, my confidence in you, and my devotion to you,—I wager these that you will win life's race and win it gloriously. My last bet-with my last coin-you will win!

"If this is good-by—good-by."

It was several weeks before he returned, bringing with him all that was earthly of one whose races were over and who himself had just been entered for the unknown stake of the Great Futurity.

Now February had reappeared, and with it came another stage of Progress. When he entered the breakfast room one morning-always to a hearty breakfast-he went first to the windows and looked out at the low dark clouds shrouding the sky and the rapidly whitening earth: it was snowing heavily. As he turned within, the bleakness out of doors brightened the fire and added its comfort to the breakfast table. While he was pouring out his coffee, suddenly through one window an object appeared; and looking out, he saw Frederick Ousley on horseback at the foot of the pavement: he was but half seen, laughing and beckoning amid the thickly falling flakes.

The doctor rushed out to the porch, and young Ousley spurred his horse up to the side of it, riding over flower-beds, trampling and ruining plants that happened not now to be in bloom. The two friends after a long crushing grip poured out their friendship with eye and speech, greeting and laughter.

Two products of that land. With much in sympathy, with no outward resemblance: one of little mingled Anglo-Saxon blood: the other of Scotch-Irish Anglo-Saxon strains which have created so much history wherever they have made their mortal fight. The young Kentucky Anglo-Saxon on his horse, blond-haired, blue-eyed, with heavy body and heavy limbs, a superb animal to begin with, wheresoever and in whatsoever the animal might end: the snow on the edges of his yellowish hair and close-clipped beard; around his neck, just visible inside his upturned coat collar, a light blue scarf, a woman's scarf, tied there as he had started by tender fingers that had perhaps craved the mere touching of his flesh: the scarf, as it were, of Lohengrin blue; for there was something so knightly about him, he radiated such a passion of clean young manhood, that you all but thought of him as a Kentucky Lohengrin-whom no Elsa had questioned too closely, and for whom there would never be a barren return to Montserrat.

Facing him, the young Kentucky Scotch-Irish Anglo-Saxon, physical equal, physical opposite: dark and swarthy soldier of the South: as he stood there giving you no notion that for him waited the crimson-dyed cup of Life's tragic brew, topped at this moment with the white dancing foam of youth and happiness.

They talked rapidly of many things. Then the object of the visit was disclosed-with an altered voice and manner: —

"As soon as you have had breakfast, Downs, I wish you would come over. Mrs. Ousley is not very well. She would like to see you."

Then he added with affectionate seriousness: "I have told her about you: how we have known each other all our lives, have played together, hunted together, slept together, travelled together, studied together. She knows all about you! I have prepared the way for you to be her physician. There was a great difficulty there-that question of her physician: you will know *that*, when you know *her*!"

A new look had come into his eyes: he stood as on the peak of experience-the true mountain-top of the life of this world.

"I will come at once."

Young Ousley, with a sudden impulse, perhaps to conceal his own sacred emotion, rode over to a window of the breakfast room and peered in at the waiting table with its solitary chair at the head. He raised his voice as though speaking to an imaginary person inside:

"How do you do, Mrs. Birney?" he said. "Could I speak to the doctor a moment? I should like to have his private ear professionally: could you pass one of his ears out?"

The doctor stooped and scraped together a snowball from the edge of the porch, and with a soft toss hit him in the face: —

"Take that for speaking to Mrs. Birney through a window! And Mrs. Birney is not my office boy. And I do the passing out of my own ears-to any desired distance."

The young husband rode back to the porch, wiping the snow out of his laughing eyes: they looked blue as with the clear laughter of the sky.

"That will never do!" he said with a backward motion of his head toward the solitary chair at the breakfast-table. "What right have you to defraud a girl out of all that happiness?"

"I am not defrauding a girl out of all that happiness: I am being defrauded. I am not the culprit: I am the victim. As a consequence of trying to save the lives of other husbands, I have nearly come to my own death as a bachelor: I have about succumbed to inanition: I am a mere Hamlet of soliloquy-and abstention."

It was the last playfulness of boyhood friendship, of a return to old ways of jesting when jesting meant nothing. But the glance into the breakfast room-those rallying words-the return of the snowball into the face-were the ending of a past: each felt that this was enough of it.

As young Ousley rode away, he wheeled his horse at the distance of some yards and called back formally: —

"Mrs. Ousley would like to see you as soon as you can come, doctor."

It was a professional command.

"I'll come immediately after breakfast."

"Thank you."

"Thank *you!*"

They had assumed another relation in life: on one side of a chasm was a young husband with his bride; on the other, the family physician.

As Dr. Birney poured out his coffee and buttered his biscuit, he said to himself that now the bread of life was being buttered.

When he reached the Ousleys', the youthful husband met him on the veranda and threw an arm around his shoulder affectionately and led him in; and when some time later they reappeared, both talked gravely and parted, bound by a new bond of dependence and helpfulness between man and man.

For the next few days there developed in Dr. Birney a novel consciousness that his interest in marriage had enormously deepened, but that interest in his own marriage had received a setback: the feeling was genuine, and it troubled him. The tentative advances into social life that he had been making seemed to have ended in blind paths; the growing ties snapped like threads upon which some displaced weight has fallen.

What he had been looking for it seemed to him that he had found too late in Josephine Ousley. Had he found her before her marriage, he would have looked at no other, nor have wavered a year. The actual significance of this was that he had encountered one of the persistent dreams of mankind-the dream of ideal love and ideal marriage with one who is unattainable.

The history of the race, of its art, of its literature, has borne through ages testimony to the vividness and to the tyranny of this obsession, this mistake, or this truth which may be one of Nature's deepest. For it may be error and it may be truth, or sometimes the one and sometimes the other. It may be one of the vast forces in Nature which we are but now beginning to observe-one of her instincts of intuitive selection which announces itself instantly and is never to be reversed: such an instinct as governs the mating of other lives not human. But there it is in our own species for us to make out of it what we can. There are men who for the rest of their lives look back upon the mere sight of some woman, a solitary brief meeting with her, as though that were their natural and perfect union. There are women who are haunted by the same influence and allegiance to some man-seen once-perhaps never seen at all except in a picture. Among the dreams of humanity about ideal strength, ideal wisdom, ideal justice and charity and friendship, this must be set apart as its dream of ideal love; and as all high and beautiful dreams about human nature are welcome, provided only we never awaken from them, let those who dream thus dream on. But the tragedy of it falls upon those who in actual life practically supplant the imagined. Let Petrarch dream of Laura, let Dante dream of Beatrice, if only the perfections of Laura and Beatrice do not come into judgment against the actual wives of Petrarchs and Dantes. Let the ideal love of Romeo and Juliet gladden mankind only as a dream of the unfulfilled.

Dr. Birney had fallen under the influence of this error, or this truth: the bride of his friend instantly filled his imagination as that vision of perfection which dreams alone bring to visit us. He was not yet in love with her, not a feeling of his nature had yet made its start towards her: but she had declared herself as for him the ideal woman-ensphered in the unattainable. As proof of this she released in him from the hour of his meeting her finer things than he had been aware of in his own nature: her countenance, her form, her voice, her whole presence, her spirit, disclosed for him for the first time the whole glory and splendor of human life and of a man's union with a woman.

As he tried to withdraw his mind from this belief and fix it upon his own separate future, he discovered that his outlook was no longer single nor clear. Something stood in his path-an irremovable obstacle. Sometimes in sleep we try to drive around an obstruction in our road, and as often as we drive around it it reappears where it was before: such an obstruction had obtruded itself across his progress.

During the following weeks he was often at the Ousleys'—to supper, as a guest in their carriage on visits and to parties: the three were almost inseparable. One night at supper young Ousley again brought up the subject of the doctor's marriage and twitted him for hesitancy: unexpectedly the subject was thrust back into the speaker's teeth: there was an awkward silence-very curious —

And now there befell the doctor one of those peculiar little progressions or retrogressions which prove a man not to be utterly forlorn. He had ceased to make social calls, and had begun to decline invitations; and so into the air there was wafted that little myth which went wandering over the country from house to house: the familiar little myth that he had been rejected. This myth of the rejected! —this little death-web wound about the unsuccessful suitor: every eligible man is as much entitled to one as every caterpillar to his cocoon.

He was with Mrs. Ousley when her child was born-he saved her life and the child's life and his friend's happiness. And in response he found that both of them were now drawing him into that closer friendship which rests upon danger shared and passed-upon respect and power.

The first day that Mrs. Ousley sat in her drawing-room with her infant across her knees the doctor was there; and as he studied the perfect group-husband and wife and child-it seemed to him that behind them should have shone the full-orbed golden splendor of this life's ideal happiness.

"There is only one way out of it for me," he muttered bitterly as he went down the steps. "I must marry and fall in love with my own wife and with the mother of my own children."

That afternoon he drove toward the stately homestead of the summer lawns and tennis matches-but when he reached the front gate, he drove past.

It was a few months after this, toward the end of a long conversation with Mrs. Ousley, in which *she* now broached with feminine tact and urgency the subject of his marriage, it was as he told her good-by that there escaped from him the first intimation of his love-unexpectedly as an electric spark flashing across a vacuum.

When he was miles away he said to himself:

"This must stop-this must be stopped: if I cannot stop it, some one else must help me to stop it."

That afternoon he began again his visits to the stately homestead of the lawns and the tennis courts; and a month or two later he drove by and said to Mrs. Ousley: —

"I am engaged to be married."

She gave him a quick startled look, thinking not of him, but with a woman's intuitive forecast sending her sympathy and apprehension on into the life of another woman.

One beautiful summer night of the year following there were bridal fights gleaming far and wide over the grounds of this stately country place and from all the windows of the house.

The doctor was married.

About a year later there reached Dr. Birney one morning a piece of evidence as to how his reputation was spreading: from another neighborhood a farmer of small means rode to his door and besought him to come and see a member of his family: this request implied that the regular family physician had been passed over, supplanted; and when the poor turn against their physicians and discharge them, it is a bad sign indeed-for the physicians.

The doctor upon setting out sent his thoughts to this professional brother who had been discredited: he would gladly have saved him from the wound.

A few miles up the pike he was surprised to meet a well-known physician from the city: they knew each other socially and checked their horses to exchange greetings.

Dr. Birney lost no time in saying: —

"If you are on the way to my house, I'll turn back."

"I'm going to the Ousleys'. Professor Ousley asked me yesterday to come out and see Mrs. Ousley: he said it was her wish."

The two physicians quickly parted with embarrassment.

As Dr. Birney drove on he had received the wound which sometimes leaves a physician with the feeling that he has tasted the bitterness of his own death: he himself had been pushed aside-discarded from the household that meant most to him as physician and man.

He pulled his horse's head into a dirt road and crossed to another turnpike and visited his new patient and went on to another county seat and put up his horse at a livery stable to be groomed and fed and took his dinner at the little tavern and wandered aimlessly about the town and started back towards sundown and reached home late in the night and went to his rooms without awaking his wife. As he lighted his lamp in the library under its rays he saw a note from Mrs. Ousley to them, asking their company to supper next evening. His wife had pencilled across the top of the page a message that she would not go.

"It is their good-by to me," he said; "when my wife knows that they have discharged me, as a woman understands another woman in such a matter, she will know the reason; and she will see fully at last what she began to see long since."

When he went to the Ousleys', Mrs. Ousley came forward to greet him at the side of her husband, and she gave him both hands. And she did what she had never done before-she tried with her little hands to take his big ones-the hands that had saved her life; and out of the intensity and solemnity of her gratitude she looked him in the eyes until the lids fell over hers. It was like saying: —

It is not your fault, it is not my fault, it is not the fault of any of us: it is life and the fault of life. As I let you go, dear friend, I cling to you.

When the evening was over and the moment had come to leave, she was at the side of her husband again; and under the chandelier in the hall she suddenly looked up to it with a beautiful mystical rapture and consecration-as if to the mistletoe of her bridal eve.

And now more years-years-years! But what effect have years upon the master passions? What are five years to a master Hatred? What are ten years to Revenge? What are twenty to Malice? What is half a century to Patience, or fourscore years to Loyalty, or fourscore and ten to Friendship, or the last stretch of mortality to waiting Love? The noble passions grow in nobility; the ignoble ones grow in ignominy.

And thus it came about that the final stage of the doctor's Progress attained dimensions large enough to contain Hogarth's most human four: for it represented that *Progress of the Rake* which sometimes in everyday reality coincides with the *Progress of the Harlot* and with the *Progress of Marriage à la Mode* and with the *Progress of Cruelty*: so that he thus achieved as much by way of getting on as may be reasonably demanded of any plodding man.

It was an August day in this same year which was now closing its record with the thoughtful days of December. It was afternoon, and it was Saturday.

Intervening years had developed the doctor in two phases of growth: he looked no older, but he was heavier in trunk and limbs; and he was weightier in repute, for he had established far and near his fame as a physician. He had patients in remote county seats now, and on this day he had been to one of those county seats to visit a patient, and had found him mending. As he quitted the house with this responsibility dropped, it further reminded him that within the range of his practice he had not for the moment a single case of critical illness or of any great suffering. Whereupon he experienced the relief, the elastic rebound, known perhaps only to physicians when for a term they may take up relations of entire health and happiness with their fellow-beings: and when you cease to deal with pain, you begin to deal with pleasure.

With a new buoyancy of foot and feeling he started down to Cheapside, the gathering-place for farmers and merchants and friendly town folk-most of all on Saturdays. As he strolled along, the recollection wandered back to him of how in years gone by-when he was just old enough to begin to shave-it was the excitement of the week to shave and take his bath and don his best and come to town to enjoy Saturday afternoon on Cheapside. The spirit of boyhood flowed back to him: he bathed in a tide of warm mysterious waters.

When he reached the public square, he began to shake hands and rub shoulders; and to nod at more distant acquaintances; and once under the awning of a store for agricultural implements he paused squarely before a group of farmers sitting about on ploughs and harrows. They were all friends, and at the sight of him they rose in a group, seized him and marched him off with them to the hotel to dinner whither they were just starting. They were hearty men; it was a hearty meal; there was hearty talk, hearty laughter. Middle-aged, red-blooded men of overflowing vitality, open-faced, sunbrowned; eating meat like self-unconscious carnivora and drinking water like cattle: premium animals in prime condition and ready for action: on each should have been tied the blue ribbon of agricultural fairs.

The hotel dinner was unusually rich that day because a great circus and menagerie had pitched its tents in a vacant lot on the edge of town; and there was to be an afternoon and an evening performance, and the town was crowded.

The doctor's dinner companions were to join their wives and children at the grounds, and very reluctantly he declined their urging to go along: as they separated, there rose in him fresh temptation about old Saturday afternoon liberties and pleasures-and there fell upon him as a blight the desolation of his own home life.

He made his way through excited throngs to the livery stable, and had soon started. On the way across town, above low roofs and fences, he caught sight of weather-stained canvas tents, every approach toward which now had its rolling tide of happy faces, young and aged. At a cross street the hurrying people flowed so thoughtlessly about his buggy wheels that he checked his horse lest some too careless child might be trodden on; and as he sat there, smiling out at them and waiting for them to pass, suddenly above the tumult of voices with their brotherliness he heard a sound that made him forget his surroundings-forget human kinship-and think only of another kinship of his to something secret and undeclared: in one of the tents a great lonely beast lifted its voice and roared out its deep jungle-cry. The primitive music rang above the civilized swarm like a battle-challenge uttered from the heart of Nature-that sad long trumpet call of instinct-caged and defrauded; a majestic despair for things within that could never change and for things without that were never to be enjoyed. Shallow and pitiable by comparison sounded the human voices about the buggy wheels.

"To make one outcry like that! —sincere, free! But to be heard once-but to be understood at last!" said the doctor.

When he reached the outskirts of the town, he met vehicles hurrying in from the neighbor-hood and from far beyond it.

It was not long before he saw his own carriage approaching; and his children, recognizing him, sprang to their feet and waved tumultuously. As the vehicles drew alongside, he looked at them rather absent-mindedly: —

"Where are you running off to?" he asked, pretending not to remember that permission had been granted weeks before, as soon as the bills had been pasted on turnpike fences.

"We're running off to the circus!"

"And what can you possibly be going to do at the circus? Children go to a circus-who ever heard of such a thing! I should think you'd have stayed at home and studied arithmetic or memorized the capitals of all the States."

"Well, as for me," cried Elsie, "I'm pleased to explain what I shall do: I shall drink lemonade and sit with the fat woman if there's room for both of us on the same plank!"

"And what are you going to do?"

"I'm going to do *everything*, of course! That's my ticket: I don't pay for all and see some! I'm going to do everything."

"Everything is a good deal," commented the doctor introspectively. "Everything is a good deal; but do what you can toward it-as you have paid the price."

For a while he mused how childhood wants all of whatever it craves: its desire is as single as its eye. Only later in life we come to know-or had better know-that we may have the whole of very little: that a small part of anything is our wisest portion, and the instant anything becomes entirely ours, it becomes lost to us or we become lost to it: the bright worlds that last for ages revolve-they do not collide.

He was still thinking of this when he met the carriage of Professor Ousley; and the two middle-aged friends, who in their lives had never passed each other on the road without stopping, stopped now. Professor Ousley got out and came across to the doctor's buggy and greeted him with fresh concerned cordiality.

"It has come at last," he announced, as though something long talked of between them could be thus referred to; and he drew out a letter which he handed in to be read; it was a call to a professorship in a Northern university. As the doctor read it and reread it (continuing to read because he did not know what to say) —as he thus read, he began to look like a man grown ill.

"You have accepted, of course," he said barely.

"I have accepted."

The friends were silent with their faces turned in the same direction across the country-their land, the land of generations of their people. This breaking up would be the end for them of the near tie of soil and tradition and boyhood friendship and the friendship of manhood.

"Well," said the doctor unsteadily, "this is what you have been working for."

"This is what I have been working for," assented Professor Ousley.

These intermediate years had wrought their changes in him also; within and without; he was grown heavy, and as an American scholar he had weight. The doctor clung for safety to his one theme: —

"You have outgrown your place here in Kentucky. A larger world has heard of you and sends for you because it needs you. Well done! But when I became a Kentucky country doctor, it was for life. No greater world for me! My only future is to try to do better the same work in the same place-always better and better if possible till it is over. You climb your mountain range; I stay in my valley."

Professor Ousley drew out another envelope:

"Read that," he said a little sadly, and sadness was rare with him: it was an advertisement for the town paper announcing for sale his house and farm.

"It is the beginning of the end," he said. "It is our farewell to Kentucky, to you, to our past, but not, I hope, to our future. Herbert and Elizabeth will have to be looked out for in the future: Elizabeth may refuse to leave the neighborhood, who knows?" He laughed with fatherly fondness and gentleness.

The doctor laughed with him: that plighting of their children!

At this moment a spring wagon came hastening on: it was the servants of the Ousley household.

"So you have left your mistress by herself," the master called out to them as they passed. They replied with their bashful hilarity that she herself had sent them away, that she was glad to be well rid of them. As the wagon regained the middle of the road and disappeared, Professor Ousley looked at the doctor with a meaning that may have been deeper than his smile: —

"She sent us away, too-me and the children. She wanted the day to herself. Of course this change, the going away, the wrenching loose from memories of life in the house there since our marriage-of course, all that no other one of us can feel as she feels it. My work marches away, I follow my work, she follows me, the children follow her. Duty heads the procession. It pulls us all up by the roots and drags us in the train of service: we are all servants, work is lord. I understood her to-day —I was glad to bring the children and to be absent from her myself: these hours of looking backward and of looking forward are sacred to her-it is her woman's right to be alone." He drew the doctor into these confidences as one not outside intimate sacred things. The doctor made no reply.

He drove on now, not aware how he drove. A few more vehicles passed, and then a mile or two farther out no more: they had ceased to come: he was entering the silent open country.

A Kentucky landscape of August afternoon-Saturday afternoon! The stillness! The dumb pathos of garnered fields-that spectacle of the great earth dutiful to its trust and now discharged of obligation! That acute pang of seeing with what loyalty the vows of the year have been kept by soil and sun, and are ended and are now no more! The first intimations also of changes soon to come-the chill of early autumn nights when the moon rises on the white frost of fences and stubble, and when outside windows glowing with kindled hearths the last roses freeze. Of all seasons, of all the days with which nature can torture us, none so wound without striking; none awaken such pain, such longing: all desire offers itself to be harvested.

There was no glare of sunlight this afternoon, nor any shape of cloud, but a haze which took away shadows from fences and bushes and wayside trees and weeds, and left the earth and things on it in a radiance between light and shadow-between day and darkness. It was a troubled brooding: and when the surfaces are quiet, then begins the calling of the deeps to the deeps.

As the doctor advanced into this stillness of the land, there reached his ear, as one last reverberation, that long lonely roar of the great animal homesick and life-sick for jungle and jungle freedom; for the right to be what nature had made it-rebellious agony!

A day to herself! She had sent them all away, husband, and children, and servants! The right to be alone with memories ... under the still surface the invitation of the deeps....

Dr. Birney's buggy was nearing the front gate of Professor Ousley's farm. When he reached it, he checked his horse and sat awhile. Then he got out and looked up the pike and down the pike: it might have been an instinct to hail any one passing-he looked dazed-like a man not altogether under self-control. Not a soul was in sight.

He drove in.

The main driveway approached the house almost straight; but a few yards inside the gate there branched from it another which led toward the sequestered portions of the grounds. It was private and for pleasure: it formed a feature of the landscape gardening of earlier times when country places were surrounded by parklike lawns and forests and stone fences. It skirted the grounds at a distance from the house, passed completely round it, and returned to the main driveway at the point where it started. Thus it lay about the house —a circle.

Slowly the doctor's buggy began to enclose the house within this circle, this coil, this arm creeping around and enclosing a form.

In spots along the drive the shrubbery was dense, and forest trees overhung. He had scarcely entered it when a bird flitted across his path: softest of all creatures that move on wings, with its long gliding flight, a silken voluptuous grace of movement-the rain-crow. It flew before him a short distance and alighted on a low overhanging bough-its breast turned, as waiting for him. Its wings during that flight resembled the floating draperies of a woman fleeing with outstretched arms; and as it now sat quiet and inviting, its throat looked like a soft throat-bared.

Once the doctor's buggy passed a flower-bed the soil of which showed signs of having been lately upturned: a woman's trowel lay on the edge of the sod: some one had been working there; perhaps some deep restlessness had ended the work. Here the atmosphere was sweet with rose geranium and heliotrope: it was the remotest part of the ground, screened from any distant view. And once the buggy curtains struck against the spray of a rosebush and the petals fell on the empty cushion beside the doctor and upon his knees. The horse moved so slowly along this forest path of beauty and privacy that no ear could have heard its approach as it passed round the house and returned to the main drive. Here the doctor sat awhile.

Then he pulled the head of the horse toward the house.

He reached the top of the drive. At the end of a short pavement stood the house. The front doors were closed-not locked. It stood there in the security of its land and of its history, and of traditions and ideals. Undefended except by these: with faith that nothing else could so well defend.

On one side of the pavement was built an old-fashioned ornament of Southern lawns —a vine-covered, rose-covered summer-house within which could be seen rugs and chairs and a worktable: some one had been at work; that same deep restlessness had perhaps terminated pastime here. Near the other end of the house two glass doors, framed like windows, opened upon a single stone step in the grass; and within these doors hung a thin white drapery of summer curtains; and under the festoon of these curtains there was visible from the doctor's buggy half the still figure of a woman-reclining.

She had bespoken a day for solitude. And now she sat there, deep in the reverie of the years.

Surely through that reverie ran the memory of a Christmas Eve when her husband had brought her home with him, and, leading her to this same bed-chamber, to a place under the chandelier from which mistletoe hung, had taken her in his arms; and as his warm breath broke against her face, his lips, hardly more than a youth's then, had uttered one haunting phrase: *bride of the mistletoe.*

Now had come the year for the closing scene of youth's romance in the house —a romance that already for years had been going its quiet way to extinction. The shorn group of them were soon to pass out of it into a vaster world: the young lover of the hearth had become the middle-aged lover of humanity.

And through the reverie ran thoughts of the other man who had been near during all this time-defrauded of her-his ideal; baffled in his desire; a man with a love of her that had been a long prayer and a madness: to whom she owed her life: this other man to be left behind here amid the old familiar fields-with his love of her ruining his home.

The doctor got out of his buggy noiselessly. He loosened the horse's check-rein without knowing what he did; and the surprised animal turned its head and touched him inquiringly in his side with its nose. He thrust his forefinger down inside his collar and pulled it with the gesture of a man who felt himself choking. He could not-for some reason-hear his own feet on the pavement nor on the steps as he mounted the porch. On one side in the shadow of old vines stood a settee with cushions; and at the head of it a little table with books opened and unopened: that same deep restlessness had ended reading. As he grasped the knob of the bell, it slipped from his hand and there was a loud clangor.

She stepped quickly out upon the stone before her door, and at recognition of him, with a smile and gesture of welcome, she disappeared within. The next moment the front door was opened wide; but at the sight of his face-with an instinct perhaps the oldest that the race knows and that needs never to be explained-she took one step backward. Then she recovered herself, and, unsupported, she stood there on the threshold of her home.

"*Water!*" His death-white lips framed the word without a sound.

He watched her pass quickly down the hall till she disappeared. Turning away, he sat down beside the small table of books in the shadow of the vines; and he fixed his blood-swollen eyes on the door, waiting for her to return. She came unwaveringly, and without a word placed the glass of water beside him, and then she passed out of sight behind him.

A long time he remained there. Close to his ear out of the depths of the honeysuckle came the twittering of a brood of nestlings as the mother went to and fro —a late brood, the first having met with tragedy, or the second love-mating of the season.

Then upon the stillness another sound broke —a plain warning to his ear. It was a scraping of the buggy wheel against the buggy, showing that his horse, finding its check-rein loosened, but being too well trained to move, had turned short to crop the grass beside the driveway.

How the homely things, the pitiable trifles reach us amid life's immensities!

This overturning of a buggy! The overturning of lives!

He started down the steps, and then midway between the house and the buggy he saw her.

She stood a few yards from him across the grass at one of the entrances of the summer house where she had been working at her needlework. She stood there, not waiting for him to come-but waiting for him to go. For years he had followed her as along a path: this was the end of the path: neither could go farther.

And now, turning at the end of the path, she meant to make him understand-understand her better and understand himself better.

And so she stood there facing him, the whole glowing picture of her wifehood and motherhood and womanhood: not in fear nor anger, nor with any reproach for him nor any stain for herself: but with the deepest understanding and sympathy in a great tragedy-and with her friendship.

Then she turned away and with quiet steps took a slender path which led to those sequestered portions of the grounds where she had left her trowel and geraniums and heliotropes. Slowly along this labyrinth of verdure, under the branches of the old forest trees, she passed. Now a shrub partly hid her: once the long bough of a rose tree touched her shoulder and dropped the petals of its blossoms behind her. Farther away, farther away, then lost down the dim glade.

The buggy crept homeward along the pike. The horse hung its head low; the reins lay on the dashboard; with its obscure sense that something was wrong it struck the gait with which it had always yielded obedience to the sadnesses of the land-and moved along the highway as behind a death.

Past farms of happy husbands and wives and children! Past fences on which, a bareheaded boy, he had once liked to come out and sit and watch people pass; or to meet his uncle as he returned home. Past the little roadside church, its doors and windows so tightly shut now during the week, where years before he had sat one morning and had shot the arrow of a boy's satire at the Commandment for men only.

Two voices for him that day-the same two that are in every man, the only two in any man: the cry of the jungle —I *will* —and the voice of the mountain-top —

Thou Shalt Not.

V. Evergreen and Thorn Tree

Four months had elapsed since that August afternoon of summer heat and passion-not a lengthy period as reckoned on the mere unemotional calendar. But changes in our lives are not measurable by days: we may spend eventless years with no inner or outer sign of growth, and then some hour may bring a readjustment, an advancement, of our whole being. The oriental story of Saul of Tarsus, made a changed man by a voice or a vision of heavenly things, is human and natural, and for this reason if for no other has been credible to thousands of men-this reversal of direction on life's road.

As Dr. Birney now on the morning of this twenty-fourth of December sat in his library, trying to make out the bills of the year, and there lay disclosed before him the book of the years-the story of his life from boyhood up-he by and by abandoned the filling out of blanks against his professional neighbors and began to cast up as at the end of no previous year his own human debt to the better ideals of his fellow-beings —and to himself. And Nature, who was grievously in his debt but had no notion of paying, Nature stood at his shoulder and pressed him for settlement in that old formula of hers: you need not have opened this account with Nature, but since it has been opened, there is no closing it. It runs until you are declared bankrupt; and you are not bankrupt until you are dead. Then of course as a business firm I shall lose what I have not already collected from you; but there are enough others to keep the concern prosperous and going. Meantime-make a partial payment *now*: payment in suffering, payment in expiation, payment in self-repudiation. If you have any funds invested in a habit of inferiority, they are acceptable: I levy on them.

One particular fact this morning had riveted Dr. Birney's attention upon the slow inexorable grinding of these mills of life.

For years the unhappiness of his domestic affairs-the withdrawal of his wife from him under his roof-had by insensible stages travelled as a story to all other homesteads in that region. In his own house it had always remained a mute tragedy: each of the two who bore the yoke of it made no willing sign; each turned toward their world the unbetraying countenance. And it must be remembered that half a century ago and less you might have journeyed inquisitively through the length and breadth of that land and have found probably not one case of divorce nor of separation without divorce: among that people marriage was truly for better or for worse —a great binding and unalterable sacrament of blended lives. If after marriage love's young dream ended, then you lived on where you were-wide awake; if all gorgeous colors left the clouds and the clouds left the sky, you stood the blistering sun; if it turned out to be oil and water poured together, at least it was oil and water within the same priceless cruet: and the perpetuity of the cruet was considered of more value to society than the preservation of a little oil and water.

No divorce then nor separation in his case; nor any voluntary vulgarization of the truth, and yet a widely diffused knowledge of this truth among neighbors, among his brother physicians, in county seats, and away down on that lower level of the domestic servants, the proudest experience of whose lives is perhaps the discovery of something to criticise in those far above them: is it not a personal triumph to level a pocket telescope on the sun?

And all this Dr. Birney had grown used to through Nature's kind indurations: all of us have to grow used to so much; and perhaps there is no surer test for any of us than how much we can bear. But in one of life's directions only-in the direction of his children-his outlook had hitherto been as refreshing to him as sunlight on the young April verdure of the land. In that direction had still been left him complete peace, because there still dwelt spotlessness.

But the father had long dreaded the arrival in his children of an age when they must commence to see things in their home which they could not understand or in fairness judge. He carried that old dread felt by so many parents that by and by the children will be forced to understand-and to misunderstand-the lack of something in the house. It was for this very reason that permission had the more gladly been granted them this year to celebrate their Christmas elsewhere; for this festival brings into relief as nothing else the domestic peace of a fireside or the discords that mar the lives of those gathered in coldness about its warmth.

And now the long expected had arrived. His conversation with his little boy that morning before the two children had darted off for their Christmas away from home had brought the announcement: the boy was at last mature enough to begin to put his own interpretation upon the estrangement of his parents. Moreover, the son now believed that he had found the father out, had penetrated to his secret; and the doctor recalled the words which had conveyed this youthful judgment to him: —

"If I should get tired of Elizabeth and wanted a little change and fell in love with another man's wife —"

There was the snow-white annunciation! There the doctor got insight into the direction that a young life tended to take! There was the milestone already reached by the traveller! That is, his son out of devotion to him had already entered into a kind of partnership in his father's marital unfaithfulness. The boy had laughed in his father's eyes with elation at his own loyalty.

These tidings of degeneracy it was that so arrested the doctor on this day. The influence of the house had at last reached the only remaining field thus far unreached; and now the seeds of suggestion had been dropped from one ripened life into new soil, sowing the world's harvest over again-that old, old harvest-of tares and tears. Hitherto his tragedy had been communicated to his own generation; now it had dropped into the next generation: it had been sown past his own life futureward.

The shock of this discovery had befallen him just when Dr. Birney had begun to extricate himself from his whole past; when he had begun to hope that it might somehow begin to be effaced, sponged away.

For although but four months had passed from that August afternoon to this December morning, a great change had been wrought in him.

When on the day following that sad August one he about the middle of the forenoon had driven distractedly into Professor Ousley's yard, he saw that friend of his youth, the man he loved best of men, the most nearly perfect character he knew among men, —he saw him sitting on a rustic bench under an old forest tree inside his front gate, —waiting for him. Beside him on the bench lay papers over which he was working-not because he enjoyed work at that moment probably, but because it was impossible to sit there and wait with empty hands-with his mind tortured by one thought, the sorrow and shame of this meeting.

As the doctor somehow got out of his buggy and started across the grass toward him, he did not look up because he could not look up at once; and he did not rise and come to meet him; it was impossible-for a moment. But then with a high bracing of himself-he came. And coming, he showed in his face only deep emotion, anxiety, distress, such as a true man might feel for another true man who had been caught in one of life's disasters. As a friend might walk toward a friend who from perfect health had by some accident of machinery tottered to him mangled; or as to a friend of wealth who through some false investment had by a turn of fortune's wheel been left penniless; or as to a friend of sound eyesight who had suddenly lost the power of right vision; or as to a friend who travelling a straight road across a perilous country had by some atrophy or lesion of the brain lost his bearings and was found wandering over a precipice.

"How do you do, Downs?" he called out, using the old first name which for years now he had dropped, the boyish name of complete boyish friendship. "Come and sit down," he said, and he wound his arm through the doctor's and all but supported him until they reached the seat under the tree.

And then, without waiting or wavering or looking at his friend's face, most of all without allowing him to utter a word (like a man aroused to the battle of a whole life which concentrated itself then and there), he turned to his papers and began to speak of the future-of the professor-ship with its new work, new duties, new services-to the going away from Kentucky: not once did he turn the talk away from the new, the future, except that when he finished he covered the whole theme by saying that the old ties must hold fast and become the dearer for the separation.

He wanted the doctor's advice, insisted upon having it, forced him too on into this future. Not a word, not a look of the eye, not a note in the voice, about a thing so near, too near.

"Now this is the end of that," he said, putting the papers away. "But it all brings up something else: the farther we go forward, the longer we look backward; and the future, this new future, has turned my eyes all the more toward the past, Downs, our past-yours and mine!"

And so he began to talk about this past. He went back to their boyhood together. He laughed over the time when he began to go to the manor house every Saturday to stay all night. He declared that he had expected the first time to starve in a house where there were no women; but to his astonishment-and relief-he had found that he had devoured things as never before. He had not been prepared to say-speaking for the boy he then was-that a woman at the table took away his appetite; but there was the fact, unquestionable and satisfying, that at the table with males only he had discovered bodily abysses within himself that had never been called into requisition! He was as frivolous as all this, winding quietly along through those happy years.

He recalled another incident: that during one of their first rabbit hunts they had fired almost simultaneously at the same rabbit. As neither could claim the glory of killing it, they had decided that at least they must share equally the glory of its pelt. And so, measuring to an equal distance from the tip of its nose and the tip of its tail, they had there inserted a penknife and severed the skin; and then, propping their boots, soles against soles, like those resolved on a tug of war, and each taking hold of his half of the skin, with one mighty jerk backwards each was in possession of his trophy! He was as frivolous as that. Nor would he ever leave this theme of their friendship, weaving about it here and there remembered tricks and escapades as he traced it down-this bond in their lives. (There were such friendships in those days.)

And so he poured out a man's tribute to a man's friendship; and then quickly with a change of tone by which we all may intimate to a visitor that his visit is at an end, he bade the doctor take his leave. But he did one thing first-one little thing: —

"Josephine sent you these, and told me to pin them on you, with her love," he said with a tremor of the mouth, his eyes filling; and taking from the lapel of his coat a little freshly plucked bunch of heliotrope and rose geranium, he leaned affectionately over against the doctor's shoulder and pinned the flowers on his breast.

Then he held out his hand as if to drag the doctor to his feet, walked with him to the buggy, pushed him in, put the reins in his palm, and gave a slap to the horse to start it.

"Come to see us, Downs," he said; "we can't have you much longer."

Truly if the rest of us had nobility enough to treat one another's failings with sympathy and understanding, there would be few tragedies for us in our human lives, except the inevitable tragedies of nature.

The way in which these two friends instead of turning away from him instantly turned toward him, sparing not themselves that they might rescue him from what now might swiftly and easily be utter ruin-this most human touch of most human nobleness wrought in him a revelation and a revolution.

On one day he had gone to the end of the long path of temptation: there was relief in that even. And on the next what is finest in human nature had come to his rescue. And both of these things changed him. Every day since had been changing him. The unlifted shadow that had overlain the landscape of his life had begun to break up into moving shadows traversed by rifts of light: a ravishing greenness began to reappear in the world. That old irremovable obstruction across his road had been withdrawn: once again there was a clear path and single vision.

But the sower may become a new character; the growth of what he has sowed must go on. And the doctor with a vision clarified and corrected now saw thriving everywhere around him young plants the germs of which he had so long been scattering. A farmer might from a field by dint of infinite patience and searching recover every seed that he had thrown forth; but as well might he try to gather back a shower of raindrops from dry clods.

And as the doctor sat in his library that morning with this final announcement to him of how things sown were growing in the nature of his little boy, it seemed to him the moment to call upon Nature for a settlement-Nature who never fails to collect a bill, but who never pays one. And sitting there with the whole subject before him as a physician studying his own case, he asked of Nature whether without any will of his own she had not started him in life with too great susceptibility to the power of suggestion. Far back when his character was being moulded, had not Nature seen to it that wrong suggestions were sown in him? Had not all his trouble started there? Was not *he* harvesting what he had not scattered? This immeasurable power of suggestion, this new mystery which innumerable minds were now trying to fathom, to govern, to apply. This fresh field of research for his own science of medicine-this wounding and this healing, this waylaying and misleading, by suggestion. This plan of Nature that no human being should escape it, that it should be the very ether which all must breathe.

Meantime out of doors the face of Nature had rapidly changed; his forecast of early morning had been fulfilled: the wind had died down, clouds had overspread the sky, and it was snowing rapidly. On turnpike and lane and crossroads there was falling the dry snow of true winter when there is sleighing.

He had given up work and had long been walking restlessly to and fro from one room to another; and now as he stood at a window and looked out at the mantle of ermine being woven for all unsightly things, at the hiding away of the year's blots and stains under the one new spotlessness, his thoughts buried themselves with getting out his own sleigh and with his trip across country in the afternoon to the homes of the sick children. But more intimately he thought of the long drive homeward from the distant county seat late that night-with his memories of Christmas Eve.

He turned from the window, and going to his office set about the work of mending the sleigh-bells. For some reason he did this most quietly lest they should send any sound through the stillness of the house. Once as a bell tumbled out of its place, instinctively he put his hand over it as though it were human and he must silence its mouth of merriment. Sleigh-bells seemed out of place in these rooms; they threw their music into old wounds. When he had finished, he put them just inside the door of the small room opening toward the stable where his man could take them away without making any noise.

And now another sound caught the doctor's ear as he was washing his hands.

It was half past twelve o'clock; and his wife had entered the dining-room to begin some early preparations for dinner, and she was alone. She wished no maid to-day, apparently, at least not yet; and as she moved familiarly about there reached his ear-very low, sung wholly to herself-the melody of a ballad.

The doctor knew it-words and music: it was the *Ballad of the Trees and the Master*. In this the poet —a Southern poet who himself alike through genius and suffering had entered while on earth into the divine-in this the poet had represented the Son of Man as going into the woods when his hour was near; into the woods for such strength as the forest only may sometimes give us: the same forest out of which humanity itself had emerged when it began its troubled history of search for the ideal.

Thus her song was not of the Christmas Tree and of the Manger when Divine love arrives; but of the tree of the Crucifixion and of love's betrayal and sacrifice ere it goes away. It was not the carol of the whole happy world at this hour for Bethlehem, but the hymn of Calvary-the music of the thorn tree and of the Crown of Thorns.

And this from his wife on Christmas Eve! —not for his ear: not for any one's ear: but to herself alone.

As he listened, with an overmastering impulse he walked to the corner of the library and stood before her picture. He noticed that in the careless haste of holiday house-cleaning to-day the servant had left on the glass of the frame some finger-prints, some particles of dust. He brought a little moistened antiseptic sponge and a little red-cross gauze, and softly cleaned it as though he were touching a wound. Then he returned to the window and watched the snow falling and heard his wife's song through to the end.

It was she to whom he owed everything. It was she who, a few years after their marriage, having discovered herself to be an unloved bride, had thrown her whole agonized nature into the one remaining chance of winning his love as young wife and young mother. Having seen that hope pass from her, she had withdrawn from one tragedy into a lesser one: she had withdrawn from him. And so withdrawing, she held the whole power of ruining him. Divorce-open separation-and his career as a physician in that land would have been ended.

Instead, she too had come to his rescue. Slowly out of that too swift and pitiless a fate for her own life, she had begun to work for the success of his: it was of too much value to many to be brought to nothingness for the disappointment of one.

The doctor stood there, looking out at the snowstorm and thinking how all the people who could most have destroyed him had spared not themselves to make him happy and successful and useful.

The dining-room doors were thrown open-he went in to dinner.

Part II

I. Two Other Winter Snowbirds at a Window

"Do you see them coming, Elizabeth?"

"Not yet-except in my mind's eye."

"Your mind's eye! Always that mind's eye! Till you see them with something better than your mind's eye, don't disturb me, Elizabeth. I have just come to the Battle of Hastings. I am going to fight as King Harold. Old William the Conqueror has just finished saying his hypocritical prayers. I am arming for him!"

"Arm away!" said Elizabeth, never interested in arming.

She stood at the sunny window of the library. With one rosy finger-nail she had scratched some frost off a window-pane, and with her face close to the clear spot was peeping out. Her fingers tapped a contented ditty on the window-sill.

A few minutes later the other voice was heard again: it came from the direction of a sofa in the room, and seemed to rise out of half-smothering cushions: —

"While the battle is going on, you might look around once more for the key, Elizabeth. Likely enough they have it hid somewhere in here. They got the Tree into the house last night without our catching them. And after they think we are asleep to-night, they'll hang the presents on, and to-morrow they'll pretend they didn't. But we can't let them go on treating us like infants, or as if we were no better than immigrants. That's what little immigrants believe! And that's how we got the notion in this country. Old William was an immigrant! But I wouldn't loathe him as I do if he hadn't been one of the hypocritical praying immigrants. He could have prayed without being a hypocrite, Elizabeth; and he could have been a hypocrite without praying; but he wanted to be both, the old beast!"

"But he stopped praying centuries ago, Harold," said Elizabeth, rubbing her long nose against the window-pane as though she had a mind to shorten it on a grindstone. "Can't you find enough in the world to fight without going away back to fight William the Conqueror? What have we Kentucky children got to do with William the Conqueror on Christmas Eve! And suppose he was a hypocrite then; he can't be a hypocrite *now*! If he went where it's nicest to go, it must have been taken out of him by this time; and if he went where they say it is not so nice, O dear! of course, I don't know what became of it *there*; it may have exploded; it may have blown him up." Elizabeth had begun her earliest study of chemistry; she disliked explosive gases.

A few minutes later the deliberate voice rose out of the sofa pillows: —

"I wish it had been me to turn the heat on him: I'd have made him sizzle! If you find the key, lay it aside quietly, Elizabeth. By that time the moon may be shining down on the battle-field where I am dead among my common soldiers, all of us covered with gore: let the king lie there with them as one of them: doesn't that sound fine?"

"Not to me!" said Elizabeth. "It sounds like nonsense: what's the matter with *your* mind's eye, I beg to inquire?"

Elizabeth was nondescript. Her hair was golden-red and as soft as woven wind. Her skin had the fairness of peach bloom when bees are coming and going in the sunlit air and there is such sweetness. Under her eyes lay a deeper flush like that sometimes seen on a child's face after a first day's sunburn by the waterside in springtime. Her own face might have been called the face of four crescents. Two of the crescents you always saw-her eyebrows, twin down-curved bands of palest gold. In order to see the other crescents, you had only to tell Elizabeth some story. As you finished, she who had been leaning over toward you slowly closed her eyes and drew in a breath as though to drink the last delight of it; her thin lips parted tightly across her pointed little teeth in a smile of thanks; and then in each cheek a curved dimple came out, shaped like what the farmers in Elizabeth's country call "a dry moon" when it appears thus set up on end in the evening sky-the water for the month having all run out.

Elizabeth's nose did not appear to have originated in the New World, but to be one of those steep Lombard noses, which on the faces of northern Italians seem to have started down the Alps in a landslide, to have gone a certain distance toward the Mediterranean, and then suddenly to have disappeared over the precipice of the chin. Across the Alpine nose was stretched a tiny spiderweb golden bridge: Elizabeth wore spectacles. The frames were of the palest gold-she insisted they must be the exact color of her eyebrows.

It was the glasses perhaps that gave to her face its look of dreaminess. But there were times when her eyes pained. (All the doctors had never been able to keep them from paining.) And this often compelled her to sit with them closed and do nothing; then her face became dreamier. But always the look bespoke an introspection of happiness. It drew your mind back to the work of those unknown artisans of Tanagra, who centuries before our era expressed in little terra-cotta figures the freedom and joy of Greek children in the old Greek life. Whatever the children are doing, they are happy about it; if they are doing nothing, they are happy about doing nothing.

Thus, as long as Elizabeth's eyes were open on the world, they found the things that made her happy, neglecting the rest. No psyche winging the wide plain ever went more surely to its needed blossom, disregarding otherwise the crowded acres. And when her tired eyes were closed and the golden bridge was lifted off the Lombard nose, they were opened upon an inner world as enchanting. For with that gift which belongs to childhood and to genius alone, as the real things of life which she had loved disappeared, she caught them alive and transferred them to another land. There also she kept all the other beautiful things that had never been real on the earth but ought to have been real, as she insisted; and on these Elysian Fields her spirit went to play. She was already old enough to realize that she was constantly outgrowing things; but as they were borne backward into the distance she turned and laid her fingers on her lips in farewell to them-little Niobe of unshed tears over life's changes. Her soul seemed to be this, that she could not turn against anything she once had loved, nor cease to be loyal to it after it was ruined or gone. As a swallow remembers the eaves whether the skies be bright or dark, the nature of Elizabeth sheltered itself under the old world's roof of love.

It was this intense fidelity of character that now kept her in her watch at the window, waiting for the two friends who were to make them four children on Christmas Eve. Once, indeed, as no figures were to be seen far or near out on the winter landscape, she turned softly into the room, and much against her will continued her search for the key that would unlock the doors connecting the library with the parlor-the dark and suddenly mysterious parlor where the Christmas Tree now stood.

There was a mingling of three odors in the library that forenoon. Into one wall an old white marble mantel-piece was built, decorated on each side with huge bunches of grapes —a votive offering by Bacchus, god of the inner fire, to Pluto, god of the outer fire. This mantel now held in its heart a crimson glow of anthracite coals; and the wintry smell of coal gas was comfortably pervasive. Making its summer-like way through the gas was the fragrance of rose geranium, some pots of which were blooming on a window-sill just inside the silvery landscapes of frost. A third and more powerful odor was that of a bruised evergreen, boughs of which had been crushed in handling, and the sap of which, oozing from the trunk, scattered far its wild balsam: the fragrance ever suggested the fir in the next room.

Elizabeth went first to the mantel, and putting one little freckled hand on the Parian marble, and a little freckled (perhaps) foot on the brass fender, and pressing her side against the Bacchic grapes (which might well have become purpling at the moment), she opened the clock and looked in. The clock key was there, and Elizabeth was used to see her mother take it out for the winding of the hours-always the winding of the hours, the winding of the years, the winding of life.

Next she went to another window where the geraniums were blooming, and looked on the sill: these geraniums were her mother's especial care, as everything in the house was her especial care; and Elizabeth had often watched her pouring water on the budding green of the plants as though the drops were bright tears: once she believed the bright drops were tears.

Then she passed on to the locked connecting doors between the library and the parlor, sniffing as she drew near the odor of the fir-sniffing it with sensitive nostril as a fawn on some wild mountain-side questions the breeze blowing from beds of inaccessible herbage. Every spring when the parlor was locked for cleaning and when children's feet and fingers must be kept from wet paint, she was used to see her mother lock these doors and lay the key along the edge of the carpet. It was not there now, however.

Then Elizabeth looked in one more place.

The library had shelves along one wall reaching from the floor well up toward the ceiling in the old Southern way. Filling the shelves at one end were the older books of the house, showing the good but narrow taste of a Southern household in former times. Midway, the modern books were massed, ranging through part of the world's classic literature and through no little of the world's new science; and so marking a transition in culture to the present master and mistress. At the other end of the shelves there was a children's corner of the world's best fairy tales, some English, some German, some Scandinavian-most of them written for little people where winters are long and snows deep and pine forests boundless.

She went to the shelf where the day before she had observed her mother put a book back into its place: the book was there, but no key. So she passed along the shelves back toward the window, where she maintained her lookout; and she trailed her finger-tips along the backs of the books as she passed the children's corner of fairy tales: it was a habit of hers to caress things she was fond of as long as they remained within reach. Once her hand almost touched the key where it lay hidden-among those old-time Christmas stories.

Half glad that her search had been in vain, she returned to her vigil at the window.

"Did you find the key?"

"No; and I'm not sorry I didn't." And then she suddenly cried: "They are coming, Harold! I see them away off on the hilltop yonder, running and jumping."

The boy sat up on the edge of the sofa. He had on a suit of cassimere of a kind of blue-limestone gray as though the rock of the land had been used as a dye; and the brass buttons of his jacket marked him as a member of some military institute, which had released him for the holidays. He laid aside his Book of the World's Great Battles, and put the hair out of his eyes. They had the bold keenness of a hawk's; and his profile was as sharply cut as though it had been chipped along the edge of a white flint.

Any historian of the main stock of our early American people would have fixed curious eyes on him. Merely to behold him was to think backward across oceans and ages to a race emerging into notice along the coast of the yellow-surging North Sea: known already to their historians for straight blond hair falling over bluish gray eyes; large bodies with shapely white limbs; braggart voices, arrogant tempers; play-loving and fight-loving dispositions; ingrained honor and valor: their animal natures rooted in attachment to their country; and their spiritual natures soaring away toward an ideal of truth and strength set somewhere in a heaven. He was an offshoot of this old race, breeding stubbornly true on these late Kentucky fields.

"They are coming! They are coming at last!" cried Elizabeth, beckoning to him.

The boy got up and strolled over to the window and stood beside his sister, most unlike her: he springing from the land as rank as its corn; she being without a country, a little winged soul wandering through the universe, that merely by means of birth had alighted on Kentucky ground. At this moment beside the grave one-toned figure of her brother the many-colored nature of Elizabeth had its counterpart in the picture she offered to the eye; for the sunlight out of doors falling on the frost-jewelled window-panes spun a silvery radiance about the golden-red of the wind-woven hair, heightened the transparency of her skin, and stroked with softest pencil her little frock of forget-me-not blue. Had she been lifted to the window-frame, she would have looked like some portrait of herself done in stained glass-all atmosphered with seraphic brilliancy. As to the forget-me-not frock, everything that Elizabeth wore seemed to cherish her; her dresses bloomed about her thin, unbeautiful figure like flowers bent on hiding it, trained there by a mother's watchfulness.

"Now I am perfectly happy," she murmured, pressing her face fondly against his. "I was afraid it would be too cold for them to come."

The boy pushed her away, and placed his eye at the small clear spot on the window-pane.

"Elizabeth," he said, squinting critically, "if this is the best spy-glass you have, you would make very little headway with the enemy."

"I didn't have to make headway with the enemy!" cried Elizabeth, rejecting his hostile utterance; "I merely wished to see my friends."

The boy kept his eye at the lookout.

"Elsie has on a red woollen helmet; and she looks as though she were dyed in gore. I wish it were old William's gore!"

The sight of those far-off figures dancing toward her had awaked in Elizabeth an ecstasy, and she began to weave light-footed measures of her own.

"Now I am perfectly happy," she sang, but rather to herself as she whirled round the room.

Her brother turned toward her and propped his back against the window and folded his arms: he looked like a dwarf who had been a major-general and was conscious of it.

"I'll not be happy until that key is found. I don't propose to be defeated."

"Oh, Harold, why can't we leave everything as it has always been, if *they* want it! If papa and mamma wish to have one more old-fashioned Christmas, —and you know it's the last, —if they wish to have one more, so do I and so do you!"

"I can't pretend, Elizabeth: they needn't ask me to pretend."

Elizabeth began to dance toward him with fairy beautiful mockery: —

"You just pretended you were dead on the battle-field, among your soldiers: you just pretended the moon was shining. You just pretended Elsie had on a red woollen helmet. You just pretended you were fighting William the Conqueror. Oh, no! It is impossible for you to pretend, you poor deficient child!"

"That's different, Elizabeth. That's not pretending; that's imagining. You knew it wasn't true: there wasn't any secret about it: it didn't fool anybody. But this pretending about Christmas and about how things get on the Tree, and that idiotic old buffoon! —that's trying to make us believe it is true when it is not true; and that it is real when it is not real! That's the way fathers and mothers raise their little immigrants!"

Elizabeth danced before him more wildly, watching him with love and beautiful laughter: "So when papa says he is Santa Claus, he is pretending! And when you say you are King Harold, you're imagining! Why, what a bright child you are! How *did* you ever get to be a member of *this* dull family?"

"I didn't expect you to understand the difference, because you girls are used to doing both-you girls! How could you know the difference between imagining and pretending-you girls! When you are always doing both-you girls!"

"Why, what superior creatures we must be, to do so much more than boys," sang Elizabeth. Her head was filled with fragments of nursery ditties; and the occasion seemed to warrant the production of one. With her eyes resting on him, she made a little dance in his honor and at his expense; and she cadenced her footfalls to the rhythm of her words: —

> The innocent lambs! —
> They have no shams,
> And they've nothing but wool to hide them.
> They cannot pretend
> Because at one end
> They've nothing but tails to guide them.

She suddenly glided forward step by step, airy sylph of unearthly joy, and threw her arms around his neck and covered his face with kisses, and then darted away from him again, dancing. With his arms folded he looked at her as a stone mile-post might have looked at a ruby-throated humming-bird.

"You promised," he said —"you promised that we'd find the key, and that all four of us would walk in on them to-night. But what do *you* know about keeping promises-you girls!"

"I'll keep my promise, but I hope I won't find the key," said Elizabeth, as her dance grew wilder with the rising whirlwind of expectation. "But why shouldn't papa and mamma have one more Christmas as *they* wish it! Of course we can't care as much for old times as they do; but be reasonable, Harold!"

"I can't be reasonable that way. Haven't they always told us never to pretend? Haven't they always taught us not to have secrets? Haven't they always said that a house with a secret in it wasn't a good home for children? Why can't Christmas be as open as all out of doors? Isn't that what they call being American-to be as open as all out of doors? It's the little immigrants who have secrets in them."

At that moment there was a sound of feet, muffled with yarn stockings, stamping triumphantly on the porch.

"Oh, there they are!" cried Elizabeth, darting out of the room to receive her guests. More slowly the gray-toned little figure with the white hair falling over his hawk eyes and with the profile of white flint followed her.

And three great spirits there were that walked with the lad that day-as with thousands of other lads like him: the spirit of his race, the spirit of his land, and the spirit of his house.

The real darkness of the Middle Ages was the spiritual night that settled upon children as they began to play about their homes and to ask the meanings of them-why they were built as they were-and the meaning of other things they saw in them and around them. The architects of those centuries designed their noblest buildings often with an eye to many of the worst passions of human nature. Toiling masons slowly put into mortar and stone exact arrangements for the violent and the vile: they built not for the good in human character, but against evil-not for a heaven on earth, but against a hell on earth. When the owners took possession, they had placed between themselves and the surrounding world the strongest possible proofs of a hostile and vicious attitude. Even within their homes they had fortified one intimate part against another intimate part until it was as though the ventricles of the human heart had walled themselves in distrust away from the auricles.

The mental and moral gloom of such homes hung destructively, appallingly over children. The very architecture taught them their first bad lessons. Lifted in their nurse's or mother's arms, they peered from parapet down upon drawbridge and moat-at danger. At the entrances they saw massive doors built to shut out death, perhaps battle-hacked, blood-stained. From these they learned violence and the habit of killing. Trap-doors taught them treachery. Sliding-panels in walls taught them cunning, flight, and cowardice, eaves-dropping. Underground dungeons taught them revenge, cruelty, persecution to the death: they might look down into one and see lying there some victim of slow starvation or slow torture. Nearly every leading vicious trait born in them seized upon the house itself for development, and began to clamber up its walls as naturally as castle ivy.

Little children of the Dark Ages! —does any one now ever try to enter into their terrors and troubles and warped souls? Can any one conceivably nowadays look out upon human life or up to the heavens through their vision!

When the Anglo-Saxon, heaven's blue in his eyes, sunlight in his hair, the conquest of the future in his brain, the peopling of the future in his loins, breasted fresh waters and reached the distant shore, he had come to a great land where he could build for the best that was in him. The story of the black slave fleeing across a Western river from a slave state into a free state, thrilling millions in this country, is as nothing to the story of the White Slave of the Ages who escaped across an ocean into a world where he became a free man. The cabins of this New World became the nurseries of a new kind of childhood on the earth. There is no possibility of measuring the effect upon a child and upon the man he is to be even of a door that has no lock and of windows that have no shutters. It was while sleeping behind such undefended doors and windows that the gaunt mated lions and lionesses on the Western frontiers of this Republic bred in chaste passion their lean cubs. Out of such a cabin without a bolt and with its mere latchstring there walked forth a new type of American man, the Nation's man, who as a child had trusted the open door in his father's house, and as a man trusted the door of humanity: nor had within himself secret nor secrecy, nor trick nor guile, nor double-dealing nor cruelty, nor vindictiveness nor revenge-the naked American, unpollutable iron of its strength and honor, Child of the New Childhood, Man of the New Manhood, with the great silence in him that is in the Great.

The birthplace of Harold and Elizabeth was one of the thousands and thousands of plain American homes in Kentucky and elsewhere that are the breeding-grounds and fortresses of the Republic's impregnable virtue. The house had never taught them a bad lesson; it had never offered them an architectural trait to which their own coarser human traits could attach themselves. It had never uttered a suggestion that there is anything wrong in the human nature dwelling within it or human nature approaching it from without. It was built against one enemy-the climate. And whenever the climate began war on the house, the children had a chance to see how well prepared for war it was: the climate always retreated, whipped in the end.

Their land was like their birthplace. The earliest generations of little white Kentuckians had good reason to dread their country-no children anywhere ever had more. It was their Dark Ages. Death encompassed them. Torture snatched them from the breast. Terror cradled them. But all that was good and great in their parents fought on their side; and through the Dark Ages of the West shone the lustre of a new chivalry.

But all that was changed long ago-changed except to history; and to gratitude which is the memory of the heart. On these plains of Kentucky no wildness any more, nothing unknown lurking anywhere: a deep strong land completely gentled but not weakened; over it drifting the lights and shadows of tranquil skies; and throbbing always in the heart of it a passion of tenderness that draws its wandering children back across all distances and through all years.

Ay, there were three great spirits that walked with the lad that day and with the uncounted army of his peers; the spirit of their race-the old Anglo-Saxon race that has made its best share of the world's history by cutting away with its sword the rotting curtains that conceal sham and superstition; the spirit of his country which moves with resistless strength toward the real and the strong; and the spirit of the plain American home-that fortress where the real and the ideal meet.

II. Four in a Cage

The four children early that afternoon were shut in the library with instructions from the mother of the household: it was too cold to go out of doors any more-this was given as gentle counsel to the visitors; their father-here the head was shaken warningly at the other two-their father was finishing some very important work in his library and must not be disturbed by noises; she herself could not be with them longer because-her eyes spoke volumes of delightful mysteries, a volume that suggested preparations for the coming Night. So they must entertain themselves with whatever was within reach: there were games, there were books; especially wonderful old Christmas tales. They must not forget to read from these. Finally she summed up: they must remember in whatever they did and whatever they said that they were American children playing on Christmas Eve-the last of the Kentucky Christmas Eves in that house!

The children thought, at least Elsie thought, that they would have a better time if they were allowed to be simply children instead of American children: and she said so. She was of the opinion that being American interfered a good deal with being natural. But the rejoinder, made with graciousness and responsive humor, was that the American back was fitted to the burden and that no doubt the burden was fitted to the back: at least they could try it and see-and the door was softly closed.

The children gathered almost immediately about a centre-table on which were books and many magazines, very modern and very American magazines, which were pleasantly lighted of evenings by a reading-lamp. The two children who were at home were much used to catching echoes from those magazines as expounded and discussed by mature heads. What attracted them all now was neither lamp nor literature, but a silver tray bearing plates and knives and napkins.

"It looks as though we were going to have something delicious," said Elizabeth daintily; and she peeped under a napkin, adding with disappointment: "O dear! I am afraid it is going to be fruit!"

Even as she spoke there was a knock on the door as though something had been delayed, and the door was reopened far enough to admit the maternal hand grasping the handle of a massive old fruit basket piled with apples. There was a rush to the door, and another protest: "Only apples, and there are barrels of them in the cellar: why not potatoes and be done with it! Entertain one's company on apples!" But the door was closed firmly, and thus the situation appeared to settle down for the rest of the afternoon.

It soon having become a problem of whether the apples should go to the children or the children go to the apples, Elizabeth decided that it should be solved in the human way; and she led the group back to the table under guidance of Elsie's eyes, which more than once had turned in that direction with a delicate, not to say indelicate, suggestion.

"I suppose it is better than starving," she remarked apologetically, adjusting her glasses in order to find the next best apple for Herbert after Harold had given the best to Elsie, and as she peeled her apple, she added with some instinct of regret that she was offering her guests refreshments so meagre: —

"How much better turkey and plum pudding sound in the old Christmas stories than they are when you have them!"

Elsie did not agree with this view. "I think it is much better to *have* them," she said.

"But in your mind's eye —" pleaded Elizabeth.

"I don't know so well about that eye!" said Elsie.

"Oh, but, Elsie," insisted Elizabeth with a rising enthusiasm, "in Dickens' *Christmas Carol* wouldn't you rather the big prize turkey were whirled away in the cab to the Bob Cratchits?"

"I must say that I should *not*," contended Elsie.

"But the plum pudding, Elsie!" cried Elizabeth, now in the full glow of a beautiful ardor; "when Mrs. Cratchit brings in the plum pudding looking like a speckled cannon-ball, hard and firm and blazing with brandy and with Christmas holly stuck in the top of it, wouldn't you rather the little Cratchits ate *that?*"

"Indeed I would!" said Elsie; "for I never cared for that pudding; they were welcome to it."

Elizabeth dropped her head and was silent; then she murmured, in wounded loyalty to the Cratchits: "It *must* have been good! Because Dickens said they ate all of it and wanted more. But they tried to look as though they'd had quite sufficient; and I think they were very nice about it, Elsie, for children who had had so little training. They behaved as very well bred, indeed."

"I don't doubt it," said Elsie. "I have nothing against their manners. And I suppose they thought it a good pudding! I merely remarked that *I* did *not* think it a good pudding! They had their opinion, and I have my opinion of that pudding."

The subject was abandoned, but a moment later revived by Herbert, sitting at Elizabeth's side: —

"Dickens had a great many more things in the *Carol* than the turkey and the plum pudding," he observed, with his habit of taking in everything; and he began with a memorized list of the *Carol's* Christmas luxuries in one heap-passing from geese to punch. "I always like Dickens: he gives you plenty," he concluded.

"Oh, bother!" said Harold, the Kentucky Saxon whose forefathers had been immigrants from Dickens' land. "We have everything in Kentucky that they had, and more besides. They can keep their Dickens!"

"Oh, but Harold," pleaded Elizabeth, "we haven't any American Christmas stories! Not one old fairy tale-not one!"

"We don't want any old English fairy tales. American children don't want fairy tales. Couldn't we have them if we wanted them? I should say so. Can't we make anything in our country that we want?"

"But the little Cratchits, Harold!" insisted Elizabeth, "we do want the little Cratchits!"

"We have plenty of American Cratchits just as good-and much worse."

The eating of the apples now went on silently, Elizabeth having been worsted in her battle for the Cratchits. But soon as hostess she made another effort to be charming.

"Mamma tells us that whenever we have anything very very good, we must always remember to leave a little for Lazarus. Especially at Christmas-we must remember to share with Lazarus-to leave something on our plates for him."

"Well," said Elsie, "Herbert and I have always been taught to leave something on our plates for good manners. But I never heard good manners called Lazarus. I didn't suppose Lazarus had any manners!"

Elizabeth's face and neck was colored with a quick flame, and she bent her head over her plate until her hair covered her eyes. She undertook an explanation: —

"I think I know what mamma meant, Elsie. Mamma always means a great deal. It was this way: long, long ages ago all over the world people had to divide with imaginary beings: every year they had to give so much, part of everything they owned. Then by and by—I don't know the exact date, Elsie, dear, and I don't think it makes much difference; but by and by there weren't any more imaginary beings. Mamma said that they all disappeared, going down the road of the world."

"But who got all the things?" asked Elsie. "The imaginary beings didn't get them."

"I suppose that is another story," said Elizabeth, who was determined this time not to be browbeaten. "Then just as they all disappeared down the road, from the opposite direction there came the figure of a man-Lazarus. Of course I can't tell it as mamma explains it to me, but this is what it comes to: that for ages and ages people were compelled to give up a share of what they had to imaginary beings; but now there aren't any imaginary beings, and we must divide with people we actually see."

"I don't actually see Lazarus," said Elsie.

"But with your mind's eye —!"

"Oh, *that* eye —!"

"Mamma thought she would give us a good send-off for Christmas Eve," murmured Elizabeth with another wound: she had been as unfortunate in her crusade for Lazarus as she had been with her tirade for the Cratchits.

Elsie and Harold had pushed back their chairs and frolicked away to a distant part of the room to an unfinished game of backgammon. Elizabeth dipped her fingers into her finger-bowl, and with admiration watched Elsie in her beauty and bouncing proportions: for she was a beautiful child-with the beauty of round healthy vegetables displayed on market stalls, causing you to feel comfortable and human. As for Elizabeth, her thinness had been her pathos: from earliest childhood she had been made to realize on school playgrounds and in all juvenile companies that very thin children win no kind of leadership: with an instinct sure and no doubt wise, children uniformly give their suffrages to the fat, and vote by the pound. Now she looked longingly at the bewitching vision of her opposite-at the heavy braids of chestnut hair hanging down the broad back and tied with a bit of blue-checked ribbon —a back that would have made three of her backs. One day while being dressed by her mother she had remarked regarding herself that she was glad she was no longer: she might be taken for the sea-serpent.

Elsie was dressed in a shade of brown that suggested a blend of the colors of good morning coffee with Durham cream in it and Kentucky waffles: a kind of general breakfast brown.

Then Elizabeth's glance came home to Herbert at her side. He was dressed in much the same shade of brown. But something in his nature transmuted this, and he rather seemed clad in a raiment that suggested spun oak leaves as in autumn they lie at the bottom of still pools when the blue of the sky falls on them and chill winds pass low. Her tenderness suddenly enfolded him: it was the first time he had ever come to stay all night: it gave her an intimate sense of proprietorship in him. She settled down into her chair-the large, high-backed, parental chair-and began rather plaintively-but also not without stratagem-having first looked quickly to see that Elsie was at a safe distance: —

"Mamma says that if you have red hair and are born ugly, and grow uglier, and are very thin, and are named Elizabeth, and no one loves you, you may become a very dangerous person. She's positive that was the trouble with Queen Elizabeth. Some day it may be natural for me to want to cut off somebody's head —I don't know whose yet-but *somebody's*. Mamma and I are alike: if we were not loved, it would be the end of us."

(To think that even this innocent child should have had such guile!) A head of chestnut hair was unexpectedly moved around in front of Elizabeth's glasses and a pair of eyes peeped in through those private windows: peeped-disappeared. From the other chair a voice sounded, becoming confidential: —

"Some time before you are grown, Elizabeth, some one is going to tell you something."

"I wish I knew what it was *now*!" murmured Elizabeth.

"You will know when the time comes."

"I don't see why the time doesn't come now."

"Before you are grown?"

"It's the same thing —I *feel* grown-for the moment!"

Elizabeth looked around again to see where Elsie was.

"I'd like to ask you a question, Elizabeth."

"I should be pleased to answer the question."

"But father told me not to ask any questions: I was to wait till I got back home and ask *him*."

"I think that is very strange! Aren't there questions a boy can't ask his father? A father wouldn't be the right one to answer. You must ask the one who can answer!"

There was no reply.

"Well," urged Elizabeth, feeling the time was short (there have been others!), "if you can't *ask* it, *pop* it! If you can't ask the question, pop the question."

And then-clandestinely down behind the backs of the chairs! And not on the cheek! Exact style of the respondent not accurately known-probably early Elizabethan.

Toward the middle of the afternoon as they played further about the room in search of whatever entertainment it afforded, they stopped before an old cabinet with shelves arranged behind glass doors.

On one of the upper shelves stood some little oval frames of blue or of rose-colored velvet; and in the frames were miniatures of women of old Southern days with bare ivory necks and shoulders and perhaps a big damask rose on the breast or pendent in a cataract of curls behind the ear: women who made you think what must have been the physical and mental calibre of the men who had captured them and held them captured: Elizabeth's grandmothers and aunts on the mother's side. The two girls, each with an arm around the other's waist and heads close together, peered through the glass doors at the vital dames.

"Don't they look as though they liked to dance and to eat and to manage everything and everybody?" said Elsie, always practical.

"Don't they look *proud*!" said Elizabeth proudly, "and *true*! and don't they look *alive*!"

But she linked her arm in Elsie's and drew her away to something else, adding in delicate confidence: "I think I am glad, though, Elsie, that mamma does not look like *them*. There is no one in the world like mamma! I am a little like her, but I dwindled. Children *do* dwindle nowadays, don't they?"

"Not I," said Elsie. "I didn't dwindle. Do you notice any dwindling anywhere about me? Please say where."

On the middle and lower shelves of the cabinet were some long-ago specimens of mounted wild duck; and on the moss-ragged boughs of an artificial oak some age-moulted passenger pigeons. The boys talked about these, and told stories of their grandfathers' hunting days when pigeons in multitudes flecked the morning sky on frosty mornings or had made blue feathery clouds about the oak trees in the vast Kentucky pastures.

Following this lead, the boys went to the book-shelves, and taking down a volume of Audubon's great folio work on *American Birds*, they spread it open on the carpet and, sprawling before it, found the picture of the vanished wild pigeon there, and began to read about him.

Observing this, Elizabeth and Elsie took down a volume of the same great man's work on *American Animals*; and with it open before them on the floor a few yards away, facing the boys, they began to turn the pages, looking indifferently for whatever beasts might appear.

Elizabeth's peculiar interest in animal pictures had begun during the summer previous, when the family were having a vacation trip in Europe. Upon her visits to galleries of paintings she had repeatedly encountered the same picture: The Manger with the Divine Child as the centre of the group; and about the Child, half in shadow, the donkey and others of his lowly fellows of the stall-all turned in brute adoration. The memory of these Christmas pictures came vividly back to her now-especially the face of the donkey who was always made to look as though he had long been expecting the event; and whereas reasonably gratified, could not definitely say that he was much surprised: his entire aspect being that of a creature too meek and lowly to think that anything foreseen by him could possibly be much of a miracle.

Once also she had seen another animal picture that fascinated her: it represented a blond-haired little girl of about her own age, with bare feet, hair hanging down, a palm branch in her hand. She was escorted by a troop of wild animals, each vying with the other in attempt to convince this exceptional little girl that nothing could induce them just at present to be carnivorous.

The most dangerous beasts walked at the head of the line; the less powerful took their places in the rear; and the procession gradually tapered off in the distance until only the smallest creatures were to be seen struggling resolutely along in the parade. The meaning of the picture seemed to be that nothing harmful could come from the animal kingdom on this particular day, providing the animals were allowed to arrange themselves as specified in the procession. What might have happened on the day preceding or the day following was not guaranteed; nor what might have befallen the little girl on this day if she had not been a blonde; nor what might overtake little boys, dark or fair, at any time. This picture also was in Elizabeth's memory as she turned Audubon's mighty pages; but somehow no American animals seemed to be represented in it: probably absenting themselves through the American desire-ranging through the whole animal kingdom-not to appear sentimental. All, no doubt, would have been glad to parade behind Elizabeth; but they must have agreed that only the sheep in the United States has the right to look sheepish.

The boys, sitting behind the *Birds*, and the girls sitting behind the *Quadrupeds*, turned the leaves and began to toss their comments and their fun back and forth.

"The wild pigeon is gone," said Harold, whose ideas on this subject and others related to it showed that he had listened with a good purpose to a father who was a naturalist and patriotic American. "The wild pigeon is gone, and the buffalo is gone, and the deer is going, and all the other big game is gone or is going, and the birds are going, and the forests are going, and the streams are going, and the Americans are going: everything is going but the immigrants-they are coming."

"Oh, but, Harold, we were immigrants once," admitted Elizabeth.

"We were Anglo-Saxon immigrants," said the son of his father; "and they're the only kind for this country. If all the rest of the country were like Kentucky, it wouldn't be so bad. And we American boys have got to get busy when we are men, or there won't be any real Americans left: I expect to stand for a big family, I do," he affirmed to Herbert as though he somehow appropriated the privilege and the glory of it.

"So do I intend to stand for a big family," replied Herbert quickly and jealously, now that matters seemed to be on a satisfactory basis with Elizabeth.

"We boys are going to do our part," called out the Anglo-Saxon to the girls sitting opposite. "You American girls will have to do yours!"

"We shall be quite ready," Elizabeth sang back dreamily.

"We shall be ready," echoed Elsie, not to be excluded from her full share in future proceedings, "and we shall be much pleased to be ready!"

The boys turning the pages of the *Birds* had reached the picture of the American robin redbreast; and the girls turning the pages of the *Quadrupeds* had reached the picture of the American rabbit; Elizabeth was softly stroking its ears and coat.

"I think," said Herbert, looking across at Elizabeth, and also of that cordial lusty household bird whose picture was before him, "I think that if a real American were to begin at twenty and keep on until he was, say, ninety, he'd be able to down the immigrants with a family."

"Why ninety?" inquired Elizabeth, looking tenderly back at him and apparently disturbed by the fixing of an arbitrary limit.

"That's all the Bible allows; then you take a rest."

"Oh, then our family didn't want any rest," exclaimed Harold; "for grandfather had a child when he was ninety-one: isn't that so, Elizabeth?"

"Oh, Harold! You've got that wrong. It wasn't grandmother, you dear lamb! Wasn't it a woman in the Old Testament-Sarah-or Hagar-or maybe Rebecca?"

"Anyhow, I'm right about grandfather! I'm positive he had one. Hurrah for grandfather! He was the right kind of American! When I'm a man, I'll be the right kind: I'll have the largest family in this neighborhood."

"Don't say that! Take that back!"

"I *will* say it, and I do say it!"

"Then-take —*that*!"

The member of the military institute received a slap in the mouth from a masculine overgrown hand which caused him to measure the length of his spine backward on a large damask rose in the velvet carpet.

They fought as two young males should, one of whom had recently imagined himself the last of the Saxon kings and the other of whom had realized himself as an accepted lover. They fought for a moment over the priceless folio of Audubon and ruined those open pages where the robin, family-bird of the yards, had innocently brought on the fray. They fought round the room, past furniture and over it: Elsie following with delight and wishing that each would be well punished; Elizabeth following in despair, broken-hearted lest either should be worsted.

"The idea of two brats fighting over which is going to have the largest family!" cried the former.

"Oh, Harold, Harold, Harold!" implored Elizabeth. "To fight in your own house!"

"Where could I fight if I didn't fight in my own house?" shouted the Saxon. "I couldn't fight in his."

"Yes; you can fight in mine-whenever you've a mind!" shouted his hospitable foe.

Then something intervened-miraculously. The boys had reached the farther end of the library and the locked doors. There they had clinched again, and there they went down sidewise with a heavy fall against those barriers. As they started to their feet to close in again, the miracle took place —a real miracle, and most appropriate to Christmas Eve. In the Middle Ages such a miracle would have given rise to a legend, a saint, a shrine, and relics.

Elizabeth, who had hung upon the edge of battle, was the first to see it. As her brother rose, she threw herself upon him and whispered:

"Oh, look, Harold! Now you'll stop!"

Through the large empty keyhole of the locked doors an object was making its way: first one long green finger appeared, and then a second, and then a third-those three sacred fingers-as old as Buddha! They made their way into the air of the library, followed by a foot or more of timber; and the fingers and arm taken together constituted a broken-off bough of the Christmas Tree: sign of peace and good will on earth on that Eve: a true modern miracle!

But the member of the military institute did not see it in that light; what it suggested to him was the memory of certain green twigs that in earlier years had played stingingly around a pair of bare disobedient legs-wanton disturbers of common household peace; and as he stood there remembering, his recollection was further assisted by certain minatory movements of the sacred bough itself in the keyhole —a reminder that the same hand was now at the end of the switch. It was not the miraculous that persuaded him: it was the much too natural! But then is not the natural in such a case miraculous enough? To take a small green cylinder of vegetable tissue and apply it to a larger unclad cylinder of animal tissue, with a spasmodic contraction of muscular tissue, and get a moral result from the gray matter of the distant brain: is not that miraculous enough? If people must hunt for miracles and must have them, can they not find all they want in the natural?

There was stillness in the library as that green bough slowly disappeared. The rabbit and the robin, the latter badly torn, got put back upon the shelves in their respective volumes. And presently there was nothing more to be seen but four laughing children.

And now it was getting late. Outside and all over the land snow was falling-the longed-for snow of Christmas Eve. And the last thing to chronicle regarding the afternoon was a reading.

The little gray-toned lad with the mop of whitish hair and the profile of white flint had straggled back to the story which had absorbed him earlier that day-The Book of the World's Great Battles; and he had read to his listeners seated around him the story of the sad battle of Hastings when Saxon Harold fell, and green Saxon England with its mighty throne was lost to fair-haired Saxon men and women-for a long, sad time.

This boy was living very close to the mind of a father who was watching the history of his country; and his own brain was full of small echoes, which perhaps did not echo very fully and truly.

"That is the kind of battle we are going to fight," he said. "England had to fight her immigrants, and we some day shall have to fight our immigrants! Because they *will* bring into our country old things from their old countries, and we won't have those old things. They are the ones that brought in this silly old Santa Claus."

"If there is a war," said the son of the doctor, "I'll be the surgeon; and I know of two salves already-one for wounds that are open and one for wounds that might as well be. It's a salve that father got in France; and they may have used it at the battle of Waterloo; that's why there were so many soldiers limping around afterwards."

"Well, Herbert," said Elsie, "it couldn't have been such a wonderful salve if it set everybody to limping."

"Well, it is either limp or be dead: so they limped."

"What I like about the French," said Harold, remembering a summer spent in France, "is the big red breeches on the soldiers: then you've got the gore on you all the time, whether you're fighting or not."

Elizabeth's mild beam of humor saw a chance to shine: —

"Oh, but, Harold," she exclaimed, "they *are* so dangerous! You know the towns were full of soldiers, and there wasn't one in the country. If a soldier is seen in the pastures, the French bulls get after them! Blue is better: then you aren't chased!"

It had come Elizabeth's time to read. She made preparations for it with the finest sense of how beautiful an occasion it was going to be: she hunted for the best chairs; she pushed them together near one of the windows where the last afternoon light from the snow-darkened sky began to fall mystically; then she went to the children's corner of Fairy Tales and softly peered along the shelf; and she drew out a well-remembered volume. Then, seating herself before her auditors, she began in the sweetest, most faltering of voices to read a story that in earlier years had charmed them all.

She had scarcely begun before she discovered that she no longer had an audience: nobody listened. Saddest of all, Elizabeth found that she did not herself listen: she could no longer draw close even to the boundaries of that once magical world: it was gone from her and now she herself loved it only as she saw it in the dim distance-on the Elysian Fields of lost things.

There may have been something of import to the future of this nation in the way in which these four country children, crowded as it were on a narrow headland looking toward the Past, there said good-by for the last time to faith in the whole literature of Fairy Land. The splendid, the terrible race of creatures which once had peopled the world of imagination for races and civilizations had now crumbled to dust at the touch of those little minds. For in the hard white light of our New World backward, always backward toward the cradle moves the retreating line of faith in the old superstitions: the shadows of the supernatural retire more and more toward the very curtains that cradle infancy; and it may be that the last miracle of fable will die where it was born-on the lips of the child.

Elizabeth's face flamed red as she shut the book. It was dead to her; but her brain was musical with refrains about things that had gone to those inner Fields of hers; and now as though she felt herself just a little alone-even from Herbert-she walked away to the piano: —

"You wouldn't listen to the story, but you'll have to listen to a song! This is *my* song to a Fairy-my slumber song! It is away off in the woods, and I go all by myself to where she is, and I sing this song to her." So Elizabeth sang: —

"Over thee bright dews be shaken;
On thine eyelids violets blow;
At thy hand white stars awaken;
Past thee sun and darkness go!

"In the world where thou art vanished,
All dear things are ever young.
I as thou will soon be vanished,
I like thee from nought am sprung.

"Slumber, slumber! Why awaken?
No one now believes in thee.
I shall sleep while worlds are shaken —
No one will believe in me."

It was the poorest, most faltering, yet most faithful voice-the mere note of a linnet long before the singing season has begun. As it died out, she descended from her premature perch and went with her repudiated book to the shelves where it must be put-not to be taken down again. In the shadow of the library and with the uncertainty of her glasses, she fumbled as she sought the place, and the volumes on each side collapsed together. Whereupon a large key slid from the top and fell to the floor. With a low cry of delight-but of regret also-she seized it and held it up: —

"Oh, Harold, the key! I have found it!"

As the others hurried to her, she said to Elsie, as though boys were not fine enough to understand anything so fine: —

"It was like mamma to hide the key *there*! She gave it to the old Christmas stories to keep and guard!"

Soon after this the children were not seen in the room. Some one came for them, and they were made ready for supper. After supper they were kept well guarded in another part of the house; and at an earlier hour than usual the little flock were herded up-stairs and at the top divided along masculine and feminine by-paths toward drowsy folds.

No lights were brought into the room where they had been playing. The red embers of the anthracite sank lower under their ashes: all was darkness and silence for the mysteries of Christmas Eve.

III. The Realm of Midnight

A quarter of a century ago or more the German Christmas Tree-the diffusion of which through-out the world was begun soon after the close of the Napoleonic wars-had not made its way into general use throughout the rural districts of central Kentucky. The older Dutch and English festivals which had blent their features into the American holiday was the current form celebrated in blue-grass homes. The German forest-idea had been adopted in the towns for churches and other public festivities; and in private houses also that were in the van of the world-movement. But out in the country the evergreen had not yet enriched the great winter drama of Nature with its fresh note of the immortal drawn from a dead world: the evergreen was to eyes there the evergreen still, as the primrose to other eyes had been the primrose and nothing more.

Thus there was no Christmas Tree; and Christmas Eve brought no joy to children except that of waiting for Christmas morning. Not until they went to sleep or feigned slumber; not until fires died down in chimney-corners where socks and stockings hung from a mantelpiece or from the backs of maternal and paternal chairs-not till then did the Sleigh of the White World draw near across the landscape of darkness. Out of its realm of silence and snow it was suddenly there! —outside the house, laden with gifts, drawn by tireless reindeer and driven by its indefatigable forest-god. He was no longer young, the driver, as was shown in his case, quite as it is shown in the case of commoner men, by his white beard and round ruddy middle-aged face; but his twinkling eyes and fresh good humor showed that the core of him was still boyish; and apparently the one great lesson he had learned from half a lifetime was that the best service he could render the whole world consisted in giving it one night of innocent happiness and kindness. Not until well on toward midnight was he there at the house, without sound or signal, the Sleigh perhaps halted at the front gate or drawn up behind aged cedar trees in the yard; or for all that any one knew to the contrary, resting lightly on the roof of the house itself, or remaining poised up in the air.

At least on the roof *he* was: he peeked down the chimney to see whether the fire were out (and he never by any mistake went to the wrong chimney): then he scrambled hurriedly down. If any children were in bed in the room, he tickled the soles of their feet to prove if they were asleep; then crammed socks and stockings; dispersed other gifts around on the tops of furniture; left his smile on everything to last a year-the smile of old forgiveness and of new affection-and was up the chimney again-back in the Sleigh-gone! Gone to the next house, then to the next, and on from house to house over the neighborhood, over the nation, over the world: the first to operate without accidental breakdown the heavier-than-air machine, unless it were possibly a remote American kinswoman of his, the New England witch on her broomstick aeroplane: which however she was never able to travel on outside New England. In this belting of the globe with a sleigh in a single night he must often have come to rivers and mountain ranges where passage was impossible; and then it is certain that the Sleigh was driven up to the roadway of the clouds and travelled across the lonely stretches of the snow before it fell.

Why he should come near midnight-who ever asked such a question? Has not that hour always been the natural locality and resort for the supernatural? What things merry or sorry could ever have come to pass but for the stroke of midnight? How could Shakespeare have written certain dramas without the mere aid of twelve o'clock? What considerable part of English literature would drop out of existence but for the fact that Big Ben struck twelve!

The children stood at the head of the stairs; and the Great Night which was to climb so high began for them low down-with the furniture. Standing there, they listened for the sound of any movement in the house: there was none, and they began to descend. Stairways in homesteads built as solid as that did not give way with any creaking of timbers under the pressure of feet; and they were thickly carpeted. Half way down the children leaned over the banisters and listened again.

Here at the turning of the stairway, directly below, there lived in his pointed weather-house the old Time-Sentinel of the family, who with his one remaining arm saluted evermore backward and forward in front of his stiff form; and at every swing of this limb you could hear his muscle crack in his ancient shoulder-joint. A metallic salute which the children had been accustomed to all their lives was one of the only two sounds that now reached them.

The other sound came from near him: sitting on the hall carpet on a square rug of tin especially provided for her was the winter companion of the time-piece —a large round mica-plated anthracite stove-middle-aged, designing, and corpulent. This seeming stove, whose puffed flushed cheeks now reflected an unusual excitement, gave out little comfortable wooing sounds, all confidential and travelling in a soft volley toward the sentinel, backed gaunt and taciturn against the wall.

The children of the house had long ago named this pair the Cornered Soldier and the Marrying Stove; and they explained the positions of the two as indicating that the stove had backed the veteran into the corner and had sat largely down before him with the determination to remain there until she had warmed him up to the proper response. The veteran however devoted his existence to moving his arm back and forth to ward off her infatuation, and meanwhile he persisted in muttering in his loudest possible monotone: *Go away-keep off! Go away-keep off! Go away-keep off!* There were seasons of course when the stove became less ardent, for even with the fibre of iron such pursuits must relax sometimes; but the veteran never permitted his arm to stop waving, trusting her least when she was cold-rightly enough!

At the foot of the stairway they encountered a pair of objects that were genuinely alive. Two aged setters with gentle eyes and gentle ears and gentle dispositions rose from where they lay near the stove, came around, and, putting their feet on the lowest step, stretched themselves backward with a low bow, and then, leaning forward with softly wagging tails, they pushed their noses against the two children of the house, inquiring why they were out of bed at that unheard-of hour: they offered their services. But being shoved aside, they returned to their places and threw themselves down again-not curled inward with chilliness, but flat on the side with noses pointed outward: they were not wholly reassured, and the ear of one was thrown half back, leaving the auditory channel uncurtained: they had no fear, but they felt solicitude.

The children made their way on tiptoe along the hall toward the door of the library. Having paused there and listened, they entered and groped their way to the far end where the doors connected this room with the parlor. As they strained their ears against these barriers, low sounds reached them from the other side: smothered laughter; the noise of things being taken out of papers; the sound of feet moving on a step-ladder; the sagging of a laden bough as it touched other laden boughs. Through the keyhole there streamed into the darkness of the library a little shaft of light.

"They are in there! There is a light in the room! They're hanging the presents on! We've caught them!"

The leader of the group was about to insert the key when suddenly upon the intense stillness there broke a sound; and following upon that sound what a chorus of noises!

For at that moment the old house-sentinel struck twelve-the Christmas-Night Twelve. The children had never heard such startling strokes-for the natural reason that never before had they been awake and alone at that hour. As those twelve loud clear chimes rang out, the two other guardians of the house drowsing by the clock, apprehensive after all regarding the children straying about in the darkness-these expressed their uneasiness by a few low gruff barks, and one followed with a long questioning howl —a real Christmas ululation! Then out in the henhouse a superannuated rooster drew his long-barrelled single-shooter out of its feather and leather case, cocked it and fired a volley point-blank at the rafters: the sound seemed made up of drowsiness, a sore throat, general gallantry, and a notice that he kept an eye on the sun even when he had no idea where it was-the early Christmas clarion! Further away in the barn a motherly cow, kept awake by the swayings and totterings of an infant calf apparently intoxicated on new milk, stood up on her hind feet and then on her fore feet and mooed-quite a Christmas moo! In a near-by stall an aged horse who now seemed to recognize what was expected of him on the occasion struggled to his fore feet and then to his hind feet, and squaring himself nickered-his best Christmas nicker! Under some straw in a shed a litter of pigs, disposed with heads and tails as is the packing of sardines-except that for the sardines the oil is poured on the general outside, but for the pigs it still remained on the individual inside-these pigs slept on-the proper Christmas indifference! For there had never been any holy art for them: nor miracles of their manger: they had merely been good enough to be eaten, never good enough to be painted! They slept on while they could! —mindful of the peril of ancestral boar's head and of the modern peril of brains for breakfast and sausage for supper. Then on the hearthstone of the library itself not far from where the children were huddled the American mouse which is always found there on Christmas Eve-this mouse, coming out and seeing the children, shrieked and scampered —a fine Christmas shriek! Whereat on the opposite side of the hearth a cricket stopped chirping and dodged over the edge of the brick —a clever Christmas dodge!

All these leaving what a stillness!

As noiselessly as possible the key was now inserted, the lock turned, and the door thrown quickly open; and there on the threshold of the forbidden room, the children gasped-baffled-gazing into total darkness! The coals of mystery forever glow even under the ashes in the human soul; and these coals now sent up in faint wavering flashes of a burnt-out faith: they were like the strange delicate wavering Northern lights above a frozen horizon: after all-in the darkness-amid the hush of the house-at the hour of midnight-with the perfume of wonderful things wafted thickly to their sense-after all, was there not some truth in the Legend?

Then out of that perfumed darkness a voice sounded: "Come in if you wish to come in!"

And the voice was wonderful, big, deep, merry, kind-as though it had but one meaning, the love of the earth's children; it betokened almighty justice and impartiality to children. And it betrayed no surprise or resentment at being intruded upon. After a while it invited more persuasively: "Come in if you wish to come in."

And this time it seemed not so much to proceed from near the Tree as to emanate from the Tree itself-to be the Tree speaking!

The children of the house at once understood that the nature of their irruption had shifted. Their father in that disguised voice was issuing instructions that they were not to dare question the ancient Christmas rites of the house, nor attack his sacred office in them. For this hour he was still to be the Santa Claus of childish faith. Since they did not believe, they must make-believe! The scene had instantly been turned into a house miracle-drama: and they were as in a theatre: and they were to witness a play! And the voice did not hesitate an instant in its exaction of obedience, but at once entered upon the rôle of a supernatural personage: —

"Was I mistaken? Were not children heard whispering on the other side of a door, and was not the door unlocked and thrown open? They must be there! If they are gone, I am sorry. If they are still there-you children! I'm glad to see you. Though of course I don't *see* you!"

"We're glad to see you-though we don't see *you*!"

"You came just in time. I was about going. What delayed me-but strange things have happened to-night! As I drove up to this house, suddenly the life seemed to go out of me. It was never so before. And as I stepped out of the Sleigh, I felt weary and old. And the moment I left the reins on the dashboard, my reindeer, which were trembling with fright of a new kind, fled with the Sleigh. And now I am left without knowing when and how I shall get away. But on a night like this wonderful things happen; and I may get some signal from them. A frightened horse will run away from its dismounted master and then come back to him. And they may come for me. I may get a signal. I shall wait. But as I said, I feel strangely lifeless: and I think I shall sit down. Will you sit down, please? Where you are, since you cannot *see* any chairs," he said with the sweetest gayety.

In the darkness there were the sounds of laughing delighted children-grouping themselves on the floor.

"Now," said the voice, "I think I'll come around to your side of the Tree so that there'll be nothing between us!"

He was coming-coming as the white-haired Winter-god, Forest-spirit, of the earth's children! They heard him advance around from behind the Tree, moving to the right; and one of them who possessed the most sensitive hearing felt sure that another personage advanced more softly around from behind the Tree, on the left side. However this may be, all heard *him* sit down, heard the boughs rustle about him as he worked his thick jolly figure back under them until they must have hung about his neck and down over his eyes: then he laughed out as though he had taken his seat on his true Forest Throne.

"When I am at home in my own country," he said, "I am accustomed to sleep with my back against an evergreen. I believe in your lands you prefer pine furniture: I like the whole tree."

A tender voice put forth an unexpected question: —

"Are you sure that there is not some one with you?"

"Is not that a strange question?"

"Ah yes, but in the old story when St. Nicholas arrived, an angel came with him: are you right sure there's not an angel in the room with you now?"

"I certainly *see* no angel, though I think I hear the voice of one! Do you see any angel?"

"With my mind's eye."

"That must be the very best eye with which to see an angel!"

"But if there were a light in the room —!"

"Pardon me! If there were a light, I might not be here myself. If you changed the world at all, you would change it altogether."

A bolder voice broke in: —

"You're a very mysterious person, are you not?"

"Not more mysterious than you, I should say. Is there anything more mysterious than one of you children?"

"Oh, but that's a different kind of mysterious: we don't pretend to be mysterious: you do!"

"Oh, do I! You seem to know more about me than I know about myself. When you have lived longer, you may not feel so certain about understanding other people. But then I'm not people," he added joyously, and they heard him push his way further back under the boughs of the Tree-withdrawing more deeply into its mystery.

"Now then, while I wait, what shall we do?"

A hurried whispering began among the children, and the result was quickly announced: —

"We should like to ask you some questions." Evidently the intention was that questions should riddle him-make reasonable daylight shine through his mysterious pretensions: on the stage of his own theatre he was to be stripped.

"I treat all children alike," he replied with immediate insistence on his divine rights. "And if any could ask, all should ask. But suppose every living child asked me a question. That would be at least a million to every hair on my head: don't you think that would make any head a little heavy? Besides, I've always gotten along so well all over the world because I have done what I had to do and have never stopped to talk. As soon as you begin to talk, don't you get into trouble-with somebody? Who has ever forced a word out of me!"

How alert he was, nimble, brisk, alive! A marvellous kind of mental arctic light from him began to spread through the pitchiness of the room as from a sun hidden below the horizon.

"But everything seems going to pieces tonight," he continued; "and maybe I might let my silence go to pieces also. Your request is granted-but-remember, one question apiece-the first each thinks of-and not quarrelsome: this is no night for quarrelsome questions!"

The lot of asking the first fell naturally to Elsie, and her question had her history back of it; the question of each had life-history.

When Elsie first came to know about the mysterious Gift-bringer from the North, she promptly noticed in her sharp way that he was already old; nor thereafter did he grow older. She found pictures of him taken generations before she was born-and there he was just as old! She judged him to be about fifty-five years or sixty as compared with middle-aged Kentucky farmers, some of whom were heavy-set men like him with florid complexions, and with snow on their beards and hair, and mischievous eyes and the same high spirits. Only, there was one who had no spirits at all except the very lowest. This was a deacon of the country church, who instead of giving presents to the children once a year pushed a long-handled box at them every Sunday and tried to force them to make presents to him! One hot morning of early summer-he had so annoyed her-when the box again paused tantalizingly in front of her, she had shot out a plump little hand and dropped into it a frantic indignant June bug which presently raised a hymn for the whole congregation. She hated the deacon furthermore because he resembled Santa Claus, and she disliked Santa Claus because he resembled the deacon: she held them responsible for resembling each other. All this was long ago in her short life, but the ancient grudge was still lodged in her mind, and it now came out in her question: —

"Why did you wait to get old before you began to bring presents to children; why didn't you bestir yourself earlier; and what were you doing all the years when you were young?"

If you could have believed that trees laughed, you would have said that the Christmas Fir was laughing now.

"That is a very good question, but it is not very simple, I am sorry to say; and by my word I am bound not to answer it; you were told that the question must be simple! However, I am willing to make you a promise: I do not know where I may be next year, but wherever you are, you will receive, I hope, a little book called *Santa Claus in the Days of his Youth*. I hope you will find your question answered there to your satisfaction. And now-for the next."

During the years of Elizabeth's belief in the great Legend of the North, second to her delight in the coming of the gifts was sorrow at the going of them. Every year an avalanche of beautiful things flowed downward over the world, across mountain ranges, across valleys and rivers; and each house chimney received its share from the one vast avalanche. Every year! And for all she knew these avalanches had been in motion thousands of years. But where were the gifts? Gone, melted away; so that there were now no more at the end of time than there had been at the beginning. The fate of the vanished lay tenderly over the landscape of the world for her.

"You say that one night of every winter you drive round the earth in your sleigh, carrying presents. Every summer don't you disguise yourself and drive over the same track in an old cart and gather them up again? Many a summer day I have watched you without your knowing it!"

This time you could have believed that if evergreens are sensitive, the fir now stood with its boughs lowered a little pensively and very still.

"I am sorry! The question violates the same mischief-making rule, and by my word I am bound not to answer it. But it is as easy to give a promise to two as to one; next year I hope you will receive a little book called *Santa Claus with the Wounded and the Lost*. And I wish you joy in that story. Now then!"

"Father told me not to ask any questions while I was over here: to wait and ask *him*."

The little theatre of make-believe almost crumbled to its foundations beneath that one touch of reality! The great personage of the drama lost control of his resources for a moment. Then the little miracle-play was successfully resumed: —

"Well, then, I won't have to answer any questions for you!"

"But I can tell you what I was *going* to ask! I was going to ask you if you are married. And if you are, why you travel always without your wife. I was wondering whether you didn't like *your* wife!"

The answer came like a blinding flash-like a flash meant to extinguish another flash: —

"A book, a book! Another book! There will have to be another book! Look out for one next Christmas, dropped down the chimney especially for you: and I hope it won't fall into the fire or into the soot —*Santa Claus and* his *Wife*. Now then-time flies!"

During the infantile years when the heir of the house had been a believer in the figure beside the Tree, there had always been one point he jealously weighed: whether children of white complexion were not entitled to a larger share of Christmas bounty than those of red or yellow or brown or black faces; and in particular whether among all white children those native to the United States ought not to receive highest consideration. The old question now rang out:

"What do *you* think of the immigrants?"

The Tree did not exactly laugh aloud, but it certainly laughed all over-with hearty wholesome approving laughter.

"That question is the worst offender of all; it is quarrelsome! It is the most quarrelsome question that could be asked. What are immigrants to me? But next year look out for a book called *Santa Claus on Immigrants*."

"Put plenty of gore in it!"

"Gore! Gore on Christmas Eve! But if there was gore, since it is in a book, it would have to be dry gore. But wouldn't salve be better-salve for old wounds?"

"If you're going to put salve in, you might use my Waterloo salve!"

"Don't be peculiar, Herbert-especially away from home!"

Certainly the Tree was shaken with laughter this time.

"See what things grow to when once started; here were four questions, and now they fill four books. But time flies. Now I must make haste! My reindeer! —"

His ingenuity was evidently at work upon this pretext as perhaps furnishing him later on a way through which he might effect his escape: in this little theatre of thin illusion there must be some rear exit; and through this he hoped to retire from the stage without losing his dignity and the illusion of his rôle.

"My reindeer," he insisted, holding fast to that clew for whatsoever it might lead him to, "if they should rush by for me, I must be ready. A faint distant signal-and I'm gone! So before I go, in return for your questions I am going to ask you one. But first there is a little story-my last story; and I beg you to listen to it."

After a pause he began: —

"Listen, you children! You children of this house, you children of the world!

"You love the snow. You play in it, you hunt in it; it brings the melody of sleigh-bells, it gives white wings to the trees and new robes to the earth. Whenever it falls on the roof of this house and in the yard and upon the farm, sooner or later it vanishes; it is forever rising and falling, forming and melting-on and on through the ages.

"If you should start from your home to-night and travel northward, after a while you would find everything steadily changing: the atmosphere growing colder, living creatures beginning to be left behind, those that remain beginning to look white, the voices of the earth beginning to die out: color fading, song failing. As you journeyed on always you would be travelling toward the silent, the white, the dead. And at last you would come to a land of no sun and of all silence except the noise of wind and ice; you would have entered the kingdom of eternal snow.

"If from your home you should start southward, as you crossed land after land in the same way, you would begin to see that life was failing and the harmonies of the planet replaced by the discord of lifeless forces-storming, crushing, grinding. And at last you would reach the threshold of another world that you dared not enter and that nothing alive ever faces: the home of perpetual frost.

"If you should rise straight into the air from your housetop as though you were climbing the side of a mountain, you would find at last that you had ascended to a height where the mountain would be capped forever with snow. For all round the earth wherever its mountains are high enough, their summits are capped with the one same snow: above us all everywhere lies the upper land of eternal cold.

"Sometime in the future-we do not know when-the spirit of cold at the north will move southward; the spirit of cold at the south will move northward; the spirit of cold in the upper air will move downward; and the three will meet, and for the earth there will be one whiteness and silence-rest.

"Little children, the earth is burning out like a bedroom candle. The great sun is but a longer candle that burns out also. All the stars are but candles that one by one go out in the darkness of the universe. Now tell me, you children of this house, you children of the earth, for I make no difference among you and ask each the same question: when the earth and the sun and the stars are burnt out like your bedroom candles, where in that darkness will you be? Where will all the children of the earth be then?"

And now at last the Great Solemn Night drew apart its curtains of mystery and revealed its spiritual summit.

Out of these ordinary American children had all but died the last vestiges of the superstitions of their time and of earlier ages. They were new children of a new land in a new time; and they were the voices of fresh millions-voices that rose and floated far and wide as a revelation of the spirit of man stripped of worn-out rags and standing forth in its divine nakedness-wingèd and immortal.

"I know where I shall be," said the lad whose ideal of this life turned toward strength that would not fail and truth that could not waver.

"I know where I shall be," said the little soul whose earthly ideal was selfishness: who had within herself humanity's ideal that hereafter somewhere in the universe all desires will be gratified.

"I know where I shall be," said the little soul whose earthly ideal was the quieting of the world's pain: who had vague notions of a land where none would be sick and none suffer.

"I know where I shall be," said the little soul whose ideal of life was the gathering and keeping of all beautiful things that none should be lost and that none should change.

Then in the same spirit in which the group of them had carried on their drama of the night they now asked him: —

"Where will *you* be?"

For a while there was no answer, and when at length the answer came it was low indeed: —

"Wherever the earth's children are, may I be there with them!"

As the vast modern cathedral organ can be traced back through centuries to the throat of a dry reed shaken with its fellows by the wind on the banks of some ancient river, so out of the throats of these children began once more the chant of ages-that deep majestical organ-roll of humanity.

The darkened parlor of the Kentucky farmhouse became the plain where shepherds watched their flocks-it became the Mount of Transfiguration-it became Calvary-it became the Apocalypse. It became the chorus out of all lands, out of all ages: —

"And there were shepherds-The Lord is my shepherd-Unto us a child is born —I know that my Redeemer liveth —I know in whom I have believed-In my Father's house are many mansions —I go to prepare a place for you-Where I am you may be also-The earth shall pass away, but my word will not pass away-Now is Christ risen from the dead-Trailing clouds of glory do we come from God Who is our home-Thou wilt not leave us in the dust-Sunset and evening star, and one clear call for me-My Pilot face to face when I have crost the bar —"

In the room was the spiritual hymn of the whole earth from the beginning until now: that somewhere in the universe there is a Father and a Fatherland; that on a dying planet under a dying sun amid myriads of dying stars there is something that does not die-the Youth of Man. In that youth all that had been best in him will come to fullest life; all that was worst will have dropped away.

The room was very still awhile.

Then upon its intense stillness there broke a sound-faint, far away through the snow-thickened air —a melody of coming sleigh-bells. All heard, all listened.

"Hark, hark! Do you hear! Listen! They are coming for me! They're coming!"

The Tree shook as he who was sitting under its branches rose to his feet with these words.

"That is father's sleigh: I know those bells: those are our sleigh-bells. That is father!" said a grave boy excitedly.

"Ah! Is that what *you* think *I* hear! Then indeed it is time for me to be going!"

There was a rustling of the boughs of the Christmas Tree as though the guest were leaving.

Nearer, nearer, nearer, along the turnpike came the sound of the bells. At the front gate the sound suddenly ceased.

"They're waiting for me!" said a voice from behind the Tree as it moved away in the direction of the chimney.

Then all heard something more startling still.

The sleigh was approaching the house. Out of the silence and the darkness of Christmas Eve there was travelling toward the house another story-the drama of a man's life.

At the distance of a few hundred yards the sound of the sleigh-bells, borne softly into the room and to the rapt listeners, showed that the driver had turned out of the main drive and begun to encircle the house by that path which enclosed it as within a ring-within the symbol of the eternal.

Under old trees now snow-laden, past the flower-beds of summer, past the long branches of flowering shrubs and of roses that no longer scattered their petals, but now dropped the flowers of the sky, past thoughts and memories, it made its way: as for one who doubles back upon the track of experience with a new purpose and revisits the past as he turns away from it toward another future. Through the darkness, across the fresh snow, on this night of the anniversary of home life, there and on this final Christmas Eve after which all would soon vanish, he drew this band-binding together all the lives there grouped-putting about them the ring of oneness.

That mournful melody of secrecy and darkness began to die out. Fainter and fainter it pulsed through the air. At the gate it was barely heard and then it was not heard: was it gone or was it waiting there?

By the chimney-side there were faint noises.

"He is gone!" whispered Elizabeth with one intense breath.

V. When a Father Finds Out About a Son

Christmas had passed, bringing up the train of its predecessors-the merry and sad parade of the years.

It departed a little changed, and it left the whole world a little changed by the new work of new children-by that innumerable army of the young who are ever usurping the earth from the old; who successively refashion it in their own image, and in turn growing old themselves leave it to the young again to refashion still further: leaving it always to the child, the destroyer and saviour of the race.

And yet it is the Child that amid all changes believes that it will escape all change.

Christmas had passed, and human nature had settled once more to routine and commonplace, starting to travel across another restful desert of ordinary days before it should reach another exhausting oasis of the unusual. The young broke or threw away or forgot their toys; the old lifted once more to their backs familiar burdens with a kind of fretful or patient liking for them.

The sun began to return with his fresh and ancient smiling. For a while after Christmas snows were deeper and dryer, but then began to fall more rarely and melt more swiftly. February turned its unfinished work over to March, and March received it, and among other things brought to its service winds and daffodils. The last flakes of snow as they sank through the sod passed the snowdrop pushing upward-the passing of the snowdrops of winter and of spring. In the woods wherever there was mistletoe-that undying pledge of verdure into which naturalists of old believed that the whole spirit of the tree had retreated for safety from the storm-wherever there was mistletoe, it began to withdraw from sight and hide itself amid young leaves bursting forth everywhere-universal annunciation that what had seemed dead yet lived. Out of the ground things sprouted and rose that had never lived before; but on old stocks also, as on the tops of old trees about the doctor's house, equally there was spring. For while there is life, there is youth; and as long as there is youth, there is growth. Life is youth, wholly youth; and death is not the end of age nor of old age, but only the ending of youth: of briefer youth or extended youth, but always of youth.

Ploughing began in the Kentucky fields, and after the plough the sower went forth to sow. Dr. Birney as he drove along turnpikes and lanes looked out of his buggy and saw him. Beside him was his son, and the doctor was busy sowing also, sowing the seeds of right suggestion. Sometimes they met child patients whom the doctor had brought through the epidemic, they stopped and chatted triumphantly.

Altogether it was springtime for the doctor for more reasons than one. There was a change in him. He looked younger and he was younger. The weight as of a glacier had melted away from him. A new verdure of joy started forth. The beauty and happiness of the country about him found counterpart and response in his own nature.

One day as the two were driving across a fine growing landscape the doctor was trying to impart a larger idea of service; and so he was saying that there were three fathers: he was the first father-to be looked to for counsel and guidance and protection: this father was to be served loyally; he must be fought for if there were need, died for. But by and by the first father would step aside and a second take his place, much greater, more powerful-the fatherland. For this second father also his listener must be ready to fight, to die; he must look to it for guidance and safety. Then again in time the second father would disappear and the third Father would take him in hand-the Father of all things.

"And then I'll have to fight and die for the third Father."

"I am not so sure about the fighting and the dying," said the doctor with a quick, happy laugh.

"And after the third Father-who gets me next? When He is done with me, then what?"

"I am not so sure about that, either," admitted the doctor. "The third Father will keep you a long time; and as all the troops are his, there may be nobody to fight: but He'll make you a good soldier!"

Thus during these days, each in his own way was putting forth new growth; and now there arrived a morning when the son was to show how well grown he was and how faithfully things sown in him were maturing.

At breakfast for some lack of fine manners he received instructions from his mother. By way of grateful acknowledgment, he laid down his knife and fork and stiffened his back against his chair and looked at her steadily: —

"I don't see what you have to do with my manners," he said, as though the opportunity had come at last for him to speak his mind on the family situation. "You've spoiled everything for us. You ought never to have been my mother. Mrs. Ousley ought to have been my mother." And then he looked at his father for approval that he had brought the truth out at last.

The doctor at the beginning of that utterance had started toward him with the quick movement of one who tries to shut a door through which a hurricane has begun to rush. Now without a word he rose from the table and grasping the boy by the wrist led him from the room.

As the door closed behind them, a loud ringing laugh was heard as though the two were going off to enjoy something together. Then another door was closed, and then there resounded through the silence of all the rooms a loud startled scream; not so much of pain but of bewilderment, of amazement, of grief of mind, of a puzzle in the brain. Then there were other sounds, other sounds, other sounds. And then one long continued sound-low, piteous, inconsolable.

The spring advanced; tide of new life overflowed the land. Dr. Birney and his boy were seen driving on all bright days: not toward the sick necessarily; sometimes they were on their way to a creek or pond to fish.

There was a tragic change in the doctor, and there was a grave change in his son. The father's face began to show the responsibility of handling a case that was becoming more difficult; on a landscape of growing things-growing with the irresistible force of Nature, how was he to arrest the growth of things in the nature of a child? And the boy was beginning in his way to consider the danger of too much devotion to a father, too blind an imitation of him. In his way he was trying to get clear hold of this problem of how to imitate and how not to imitate. Something was gone between them; not affection, but peace. Each was puzzled by the other, and each knew the other was puzzled. How completely they jerked shining fish out of the lucent water; but as each dropped his hook into the sea of character, neither felt assured what he might draw up. At times in the doctor's eyes there was an expression too sad to be seen in any father's; and in the boy's was the look of the first deterioration in life-the defeat of being punished for what he thought was right.

Late one cold rainy afternoon in April there were several buggies in Dr. Birney's yard, three of them belonging to physicians called into consultation from adjoining county seats. One of the phenomena which baffle the science of medicine had appeared on the doctor's threshold-the sporadic case. Long after an epidemic is over, by an untraceable path infection arrives. It is quite as if a bird that cannot migrate should be found unearned on the opposite coast of a sea.

There was little need of the consultation; the disease was well known, the treatment was that agreed upon by the profession; Dr. Birney himself was the most successful practitioner. A well-known disease, an agreed-upon treatment-but a rate of mortality.

Others came, not called: friends, neighbors, members of his Masonic order. During all these years he had slowly won the heart of the whole people, and now it turned to him.

The doctor watched the progress of the case like one who must now bring to bear the resources of a lifetime and of a life; who must cast the total of skill and of influence on the side of the vital forces.

As the disease ran on in its course, to him it became more and more a question of how the issue would turn upon so-called little things, as the recovery of a patient is probably sometimes secured by merely turning him from side to side, from back to stomach.

It was his problem how to drop into one scale or the other scale of the childish balances some almost imponderable weight, as when good tidings arriving save a life, as when bad news held back saves a life; as when the removal of an injustice from a sensitive spirit saves a life; as when the healing of a wound of the mind in the very extremity saves a life.

He felt that before him now were oscillating those delicate balances, never quite in equilibrium: a joy dropped into one, a sorrow dropped into the other-some pennyweight of new peace, some grain of additional worry! The shadows collected on one side, sunbeams gathered on the other.

"Now then," he thought within himself, "now then is the hour when I must be sunlight to him-not shadow!"

He watched the look in his little boy's eyes; he noted the presence of things weighing heavily. There was a tangle, a perplexity, a tossing of the head from side to side on the pillow-as if to turn quickly away from things seen.

"Do I cast a light on him? Do I cast a shadow? Does my presence here by him bring tranquillity, rest, sound sleep? As he sees into me, does what he sees strengthen? Was his chastisement that morning a sunbeam? It had not struck him like a sunbeam; it had not fallen in that way! The chill in the house all these years-had that been vital warmth to him?"

There now came out the meaning of all that exaggeratedly careful training: the exercise, the outdoor life, everything: it was the attempt to develop robust health on a foundation not robust: everything went back to the poor start: each child had been born delicate.

At intervals during the illness there were bits of talk. One night the doctor rose from the bedside and brought a glass of pure fresh water and administered a spoonful and watched the swallowing and the expression: —

"Does it taste bitter?"

"Pretty bitter. You can't say that I didn't take your nasty old doses, can you?"

"Don't talk! You mustn't talk."

"I'd feel better if I did talk-if I could get it out of me."

"Then talk! What is it? Out with it!"

But the face was jerked quickly away with that motion of wishing to look in another direction. Some nights there was delirium. Through the brain rolled clouds of fantasies: —

"...If I knew how it comes out between you and Mrs. Ousley...."

On these dark rolling clouds the father tried to throw a beam of peace: and it was no moment to hold back any of the truth: —

"It is all over!... There is nothing of it."

"I wish I had known it sooner: it bothered me...."

At another time more fantasies: —

"...Not on the cheek! You're no father of mine if it's on the cheek...."

At another time: —

"...Suppose I never grow up and Elizabeth does. How is that? I wouldn't like that. How do you straighten that out?"

"I can't straighten that out."

"Then I can't straighten it out, either."

"So young-so young!" muttered the doctor. "I was pretty old!"

One warm night the doctor walked out of doors. The south wind blew softly in his face, lifting his hair.

All round the house in yard and garden and farther away in the woods and fields everything was growing. It was a night when the earth seemed given up to the festival of youth: it was the hour of youth: of its triumph in Nature.

Little aware of where his feet carried him, he was now in the garden and now in the yard. And in the garden, low down, how sturdy little things were growing: the little radishes, the young beets, the beans-those children of the earth, flawless in their descent and environment-with what unarrestable force they were growing! Afterwards in the yard he passed some beds of lilies of the valley-most delicate breath of all flowers: how fragile but how strong, how safe in their unsullied parentage, in their ample wedlock!

All about the house the steady rush of the young! And within it-as a mausoleum-the youth of all youth for him-stopped!

Most obedient and well-trained and irresponsible Death! Thou hast no grudge against us nor bearest toward any of us malice nor ill-will! Thou stayest away as long as thou canst and never comest till thou must! Thou visitant without will of thine own! Quickening Death, that also givest to the will of another not the shock of death, but the shock of new life!

There loomed in the darkness before the doctor as he wandered about a true picture: an ancient people in an ancient land weighed upon by their transgressions which they could neither transfer to one another nor lay upon mother earth. So once a year one of them in behalf of himself and the rest chose an exemplar of their faithful flocks and herds, and folding his hands upon its head laid upon it the burden of guilt and shame, and then had it led out of the camp-to wild waste places where no one dwelt —*"to a land not inhabited."*

...And now he had sent away his son into the eternal with his own life faults and failings on him....

He turned back into the house-passed through the sick room-passed through his library, passed the portrait of his wife in her bridal veil-passed down the hall-knocked at her door and opened it wide and stood in the opening: —

"...My wife, I have come to you...! Will you come to him...?"

VI. Living Out the Years

An afternoon of early summer, at the edge of a quiet Kentucky town, on the slope of a grassy hillside within one of those dreamy enclosures where our earthly dreams are ended, the sunlight began to descend slantingly for the first time-as on white silvery wings-upon a newly placed memorial for a child. Across the top of the memorial was carved a single legend hoary with the guilt and shame of men and women of centuries long since gone. Beside the memorial stood a young evergreen as the living forest substitute of him sleeping below: it was of about his age and height. The ancient stone with its legend of atonement and the young tree thus brought together stood there as if the offending and the innocent had come to one of their meeting-places —and in life they meet so often.

Tree and mound and marble stood within an open enclosure of turf encircled at a score of yards by old evergreens touching one another.

Early in the afternoon two of these evergreens had some of their lower interlapping boughs softly pushed apart, and into the open space there stepped excitedly a frail little figure in a frock of forget-me-not blue. Just inside the boughs which folded behind her like living doors so that she was screened from view, she hesitated for a moment and looked about her for the dreaded spot which she knew she was doomed to find. Having located it, she advanced with uncertain footsteps as though there could be no straight path for her to the scene of such a loss.

When she reached it, she sat hurriedly down, dropped her bouquet on the grass beside herself, jerked off her spectacles and pressing her hands to her eyes, burst into an agony of weeping. Long she sat there, helpless in her anguish. Once holding her hand before her eyes, she drew from her pocket a fresh handkerchief; she had brought two: she knew her tears would be many.

At last she dried her red swollen eyes and brushed back from her temples the long sunny strands of wind-woven hair; she put on her glasses and picked up her little round brilliant country picnic bouquet; and with quivering lips and quivering nostrils looked where she must place it. With tear-wet forefinger and thumb she forced the flowers apart on one side and peeped at the card pushed deep within within —"From Elizabeth."

She got up then and went slowly away, fading out behind the pines like a little wandering strip of heaven's remembering blue.

Later in the afternoon the sound of slowly approaching wheels sounded on the gravel of the drive that wound near: then a carriage stopped. A minute afterwards there appeared within the open enclosure a woman in black, thickly veiled, bringing an armful of flowers. Some yards behind her a man followed in deep mourning also, bareheaded, his hat in his hand at his side-the soldierly figure of a man squaring himself against adversity, but stricken and bowed at his post. They did not advance side by side as those who walk most in unison when they are most bereaved and draw closer together as fate draws nearer.

When she reached the mound, she turned toward him and waited; and when he came up, without a word she held the flowers out to him. She held them out to him with silence and with what a face under her veil-with what a look out of the wife's and mother's eyes-there was none to see. He gently pushed the flowers back toward her, mutely asking of her some charity for the sake of all; so that, consenting, she turned to arrange them. As she did so, she became conscious at last of what hitherto she had perceived with her eyes only: the happy little bouquet of a child left on the sod. And suddenly there fell upon her veil and hung enmeshed in it some heavy tears, of which, however, she took no notice. But she disposed the flowers so that they would not interfere with-not quite reach to-that token of a child's love which had never known and now would never know time's disillusion or earth's disenchantment.

When she had finished, she remained standing looking at it all. He moved around to her side; and they both with final impulse let their eyes meet upon the ancient line chiselled across the marble: —

"Unto a Land Not Inhabited."

He broke the silence: —

"I chose that for him: it is the truth: he has been sent away, bearing more than was his."

She looked at it a long time, and then bowed as if to set the seal of her judgment upon the seal of his judgment. And, moved by some pitiless instinct to look at things as they are, —the discipline of her years, —with a quiet resolute hand she lifted her veil away from her face. It was a face of that proud and self-ennobled beauty that anywhere in the world gives to the beholder of it a lesson in the sublimer elements of human character. There was no feature of reproach nor line nor shadow of bitterness, but the chastened peace of a nature that has learned to live upon itself, after having first cast itself passionately upon others; and that indestructible strength which rests not upon what life can give, but upon what life cannot take away: she stood revealed there as what in truth she was-heroic daughter of the greater vanished people.

She dropped her veil and turned away toward the carriage. He drew to her side and once-hesitatingly, desolately-he put his arm around her. She did not yield, she did not decline; she walked with him as though she walked alone. During all the barren bitter years she had not been upheld by his arm: her staff and her support had been her ideal of herself and of her people-after she had faced the ruined ideal of their lives together and her lost ideal of him. It was yet too soon for his arm-or it was too late altogether.

He withdrew it; and he continued to walk beside her as a man who has lost among women both her whom he had most wished to have and her whom he might most have had. And so they passed from the scene.

But throughout that long obscurity amid which we are appointed to pass our allotted years, it is not the order of nature that all stars within us should rise at once. There are some that are seen early, that move rapidly across our sky, and are beheld no more-youth's flaming planets, the influence of which upon us often leaves us doubting whether they were baneful or benign. There are other lights which come out to shine upon our paths and guide us later; and, thanks be to nature, until the very last new stars appear. Those who early have left them they love can never know what late radiance may illumine the end of their road. And only those who remain together to the end can greet the last splendid beacons that sometimes rise above the horizon before the dawn-the true morning stars of many a dark and troubled life.

They had half their lives before them: they were growing, unfolding characters; perhaps they were yet to find happiness together. She had loved him with a love too single and complete, and she loved him yet too well, to accept anything from him a second time less than everything. Happiness was in store for them perhaps-and more children.

The working out of this lay with them and their remaining days.

But for the doctor one thing had been worked out to the end: that year by year he was to drive along turnpikes and lanes-alone. That every spring he was to see the sower go forth in the fields; that with his whitening hair he was to watch beside the beds of sick children; and often at night under his lamp to fall asleep with his eyes fixed upon The World's Path of Lessening Pain.

When the two were gone, it was a still spot that afternoon with the sunlight on the grass. As the sun began to descend, its rays gradually left the earth and passed upward toward the pinnacles of the pines; and lingering on those summits awhile, it finally took its flight back to the infinite. Twilight fell gray; darkness began to brood; objects lost their outlines. The trees of the enclosure became shadows; these shadows in time became as other realities. The sturdy young evergreen planted beside the boy as his forest counterpart, having his shape and size, now stood there as the lad himself wrapped in his overcoat-the crimson-tipped madcap little fellow who had gambolled across the frozen fields that windy morning toward his Christmas Festival.

In this valley of earth he stood there holding upright for all to see the slab on which was to be read his brief ended tale: —

"Unto a Land Not Inhabited."